Return Of T

C000130158

Return Of The Bloodstone

Return Of The Bloodstone

The Dark Realms Series of books are written and created by M.D.Nixon

About The Author

Born in England but growing up in Canada before moving back to his birth country as a young adult. A Father and a Grandfather who hopes he can succeed in bringing fictional adventure to the world in the form of his novels. An admirer of fantasy adventure stories, always wanting to bring something to those of similar interest, He created The Dark Realms series to give all an escape from reality and allowing your imagination to be drawn into a Fantasy Adventure where you feel part of the journey. A story line that he hopes to continue through many books.

Return Of The Bloodstone

The Dark Realms Series

Book 1 The Pearl Of Souls

Book 2 Return Of The Bloodstone

Book 3 The Ancient Scrolls

Return Of The Bloodstone

Return Of The Bloodstone

Introduction

One year had passed since the Return of Blaine. The world had changed and he had changed it. We have changed, we have had to change to live in this new world. Some of the lands which were once fruitful are now plagued with anger, hatred and disease. Rivers that were once flowing clear, now run red with the blood of the Innocent. More anger, hate and violence is now in our world. With the one we lost and the one we still hold faith in, we will fight for ourselves and others in our world. Blaine had changed the face of the lands, he has changed them to meet what he desires to be the new world, his new world. Magic has once again returned to the world and along with it creatures of darkness have emerged. But this change has also created others, those who will fight against the darkness. Great warriors and masters of light now also fight against the dark masters and their demon horde. The masters of light now have help from the common folk, they are helping to seek out the magic gemstones. The gemstones that will help in this fight against the evil that is growing in size and power. All are now in a race against time, can the evil that has returned be stopped? What new challenges does this bring to our world? The Bloodstone is one that will change this fight, either for the better or for the worse, depending on who returns it to our world.

Return Of The Bloodstone

The Dark Realms

Return Of The Bloodstone

Chapters

Return Of The Bloodstone

Chapter 1

It's said that time heals all wounds. If this is true then why for over a year has Krissy been full of such pain and hate, why have both Sloan and Athian been focussed on themselves and avoiding others when possible and why do I Mickel still hate myself for what happened to my father and all of us.

I've kept blaming myself for everything that happened to my father and my friends. I trusted the one I believed in the most, only to be fooled, I believed that I was doing the right thing. I thought we had saved my father and prevented the evil from being unleashed amongst our world. But no, it was not to be, it was the complete opposite. I found the pearl of souls and I threw it into the mirror which unleashed the evil that we must all now face.

After we escaped the channelling room we found ourselves in a wooded area just north of the wastelands, we were on the south side of the mountains. This is where we have settled ourselves and this is where we try to live life as normal as we can. It appears to be good here, there's not much wild life but there's enough to survive, there's good shelter from the elements and it's a good safe distance from Paradise.

During our time here we have all noticed that our world has started to change. Far in the distance we could see the large black clouds that were constantly looming in the southern skies. They never seemed to disappear, only ever growing and covering more of the land in darkness. Even though these clouds were far from us we could clearly see the lightning that striking down from them, occasionally we could also hear the rumbling of thunder. If we could hear it from here I couldn't imagine how loud it would be directly beneath them. Occasionally some of the clashes of thunder were so loud that they even made Sloan feel uneasy.

I remember when we first settled here that we once decided we would try to travel back down south, heading through the wastelands and the swamp once again, but as we travelled further south and we had better vision of what was happening to the world we were heading towards, we thought it would be best if we stayed away and kept ourselves at a safe distance.

Many people were fleeing the south and heading north for safety. They would often make their way to our settlement. We met many different types of people, city folk, villagers and even a few lords. Even though they were all from different backgrounds they all had one thing in common, they were all fleeing from the south in fear. Fear of what they had saw and what they had been through, it was the fear of the new world. Nearly everyone we met looked like they had just crawled through the ashes of a fire. All blistered, dirty and covered in a black smut.

We didn't just ignore them, if they needed support we helped them. Most of them decided to stay here with us, we helped them to survive and in return they helped us. They helped us to build our new home, they were willing to help us defend it if they needed to, together we built this new settlement.

We knew that Blaine was still out there in our world and with the way that the south was changing it was a sign that his powers were surely growing. With Davos and Delia being his loyal followers we were sure that they also would have grown stronger. They sought to control what they could before Blaine's return and now he's here in the world they would no doubt want more power from their master. We heard tales from the common folk that the city guards took every opportunity they could to attack the villages for their belongings, food or just for the want of spilling innocent blood. This forced thousands to flee the city and the surrounding areas, out of all these people that escaped the south only a few hundred had made it through to us safely. With the new evil that was now in the south many of the people who fled from there weren't prepared or equipped properly to make it safely through the swamp or the wastelands. Only the strongest of them survived, the old, the weak and some of the young were taken by what resides in them.

Those that did survive their travel north told us of many different stories, all different things that were happening in the south. They told us how Blaine had changed the city's whole appearance. Its once shiny walls were now all covered in large black roots that were choking the once beautiful exterior of the city. Some even explained how a large crevice had opened up in the city and it was constantly fluming out a thick black smoke. It was this black smoke that was changing the very appearance of the skies. They even went on to say that from this crevice that Blaine had opened managed to release beasts and demons to do his bidding. I'm not sure what he could have been summoning in to our world but I was certain that we had to prepare for the worst.

Even with all these people now with us there weren't many true fighters amongst them. Most though were willing to learn fighting skills in order to defend themselves and those amongst us. Any that weren't able to fight had other skills that we put to use, skills such as house building, hunting or weapon forging. The forgers came in especially useful, they had good experience and they were able to forge us new weapons along with other much needed items.

I spent a lot of time training and learning how to fight, how to better defend myself and my friends. Krissy was my instructor, she was the only person that could really teach us all how to properly defend ourselves. She spent allot of time with me, ensuring that I was prepared to a high level of fighting skill, so should the time ever come then I would be prepared. I never really knew how much of a good fighter she was until I started my training with her. Day after day she put me through pain and punishment but I knew that it was all for the better good.

After a few months of hard training I was at a level good enough that I could teach the common folk how to fight, after all we couldn't leave it all to Krissy. Overall, most of the common folk that sought refuge here with us had nothing, so anything we could do to help them gave everyone hope. After the incident in paradise, Athian had a few problems with some of the injuries to his neck, he tried to hide it and keep it secret from us but he didn't hide it very well, we could all see that he was struggling to freely move his neck and he always appeared to be in pain and discomfort. The best way that we could help him was by getting Sloan to heal him. It took us a while to get Sloan to agree to it but eventually he did it. Athian had some bad injuries and he was healed with strong magic, because of this he had gained some magical abilities, just as it did to Sloan when he was healed. Athian was no where near the level of magic that Sloan was but this new acquisition made him feel like he had a purpose in life, something to focus his thoughts on and a reason to continue.

During the day time he was at Sloan's side constantly. He kept learning and developing himself, listening with so much focus, something I had never seen him do before. But It was good to see him keeping himself active and busy. He would usually get bored of things easily and just give up on them, but not this time. Sloan had managed to heal all his wounds himself. Once he was fully healed he was constantly reading from the book of magic. He was learning all he could from it to make himself more powerful. He wasn't able to read the whole book as some of the symbols and languages written in it were unknown to him. I could often hear him complaining as many of the pages were blank with nothing on them. He wasn't sure why it had blank pages but this seemed to annoy him. He didn't let it stop him though and he studied all that he could, wanting to ensure that his mind was at a much higher level of magical understanding. After a few months he was able to speak many more languages and understood so much more on how to cast spells and incantations with just the movement of his hands or thought of mind. It was quite intriguing to watch, we hadn't seen him change to the wolf for a long time. He did transform a few times but each time he did this all it managed to do was scare people away. I suppose they felt that they were safer away from any form of magic and didn't want to be around it.

We managed to build several defences into the south side of the settlement and along the foot hills of the mountains. We knew that with defences up and around the settlement that we would have some sort of physical form protecting us. Slightly up into the mountains we found some old mine entrances, they all appeared to be closed off but we eventually managed to re-open them. I remember the elders telling us of mines in the mountains, but these were from the old world and had apparently been left abandoned hundreds of years ago. They use to tell us that the mines were once occupied by dwarves. We've never seen a dwarf but according to some people here in the mountain foothills and the surrounding woods there are still some that live here. It's said that they stay hidden from sight of all other's and keep to themselves. Once we cleared the mine entrances we were able to dig and mine minerals for our forgers. They used what we could find to create weapons, shields and defensive wall spikes.

One day It was late in the evening and we were all sat around the camp fire talking. We were mostly talking about what we were going to do about the ever growing dark cloud in the south and what we would do should it ever reach us. We knew that it was only a dark cloud in the sky but it's what moved along with it on the ground that we feared. Discussions between us went on well into the night. Apart from ourselves speaking all we could hear was the crackling of wood as it burnt on the fire and the sound of the night animals as they moved around in the bushes. I told them all that I thought we were ready, I thought we were ready to head out of the settlement and seek more support in preparation for what would eventually find us. As I said this Athian blurted out "I'm not Ready." "You are ready Athian, I'm ready, we are all ready." Krissy was looking at me and agreed "We couldn't stay in one area and do nothing, we needed to find more support." Sloan was sat in deep concentration, just staring into the fire. He sat upon his log bench and looked across over the fire at us, he waved his hand across the fire and the flames reduced to smouldering cinders. As he did this he clearly told us, "There's nothing more I can learn here, but these people need our protection. We can't just leave them." Mickel agreed and understood what Sloan was saying but he had to enforce the fact that they didn't have time to sit and wait doing nothing. He looked back at Sloan with anger in his eyes "My Father is gone, It's been a whole year and I fear that if we wait any longer then he will be lost to Blaine completely, that's if he hasn't t already been completely taken. I need to know if he's completely gone or not." None of them could respond to what Mickel had said, they all sighed and nodded their heads in agreement.

Sloan once again waved his hand over the fire only this time the flames rose high, bringing with them much needed warmth. Krissy looked at them all before speaking "well it's late, it appears that we are all in agreement and we must do something, let's talk about it again in the morning." She stood to her feet and just before heading back to her sleeping area she dusted herself down. She didn't like sleeping in the small houses or huts that we built, she preferred to be sleeping in her own self made safe area. At the edge of settlement there was a large rock with a small opening that went into the ground, she preferred to stay there. This allowed her to have an advance vision and hear anything that was heading our way. With Krissy being of a small physique she managed to hide there quite easily without being seen. She would often try to scare us as we walked past that area, as we would pass she would jump out and scream at us. I'm sure it was her own little way of humouring herself.

Once Krissy had left the camp fire we all went off to our beds and tried to settle the best that we could. Ever since leaving the city we were all very cautious of resting for too long. We were constantly weary for our own safety and now we had others to look out for also so we had to be extra vigilant. None of us slept for more than four hours at any one time. This was our way of ensuring we were prepared for anything that would come our way.

Sloan walked away from the camp fire first and as he did this he moved his hand across each burning torch, extinguishing them as he passed them. Athian then left the camp-fire and quickly moved past Sloan, he was trying to do the same thing with his hands but was unable to do so. I went off to my bed thinking that the next few days, weeks or even months were going to be tough, tougher than what we had already been through.

It didn't feel like a long sleep and morning was soon with us. I woke up to the sound of people talking and preparing themselves for their day. The hunters were always the first ones to head out as they had long days ahead of them. They would normally bring back a good haul of rabbits and the occasional warthog. As we had no access to the open seas any fish that we caught had to come from the closest river. But as of late the amount of fish or meat that we required was becoming more difficult to obtain. This should have been a warning sign to us that the lands were changing and we were allowing too many people into the settlement.

I quickly readied myself for the day ahead. I didn't ever think that I would be putting daggers and a sword around my waist. I could hear Athian and Sloan practising small magic spells outside my hut. I heard Sloan speaking "No No No Athian, you have to believe it with your mind, heart and soul. You have to feel it within yourself." Athian was doing well with what Sloan had managed to teach him but he always tried to over do it, most of the time he made it much harder for himself to complete any spell.

As I could hear them up and about, I walked out of my hut "Morning all, how is everyone today." Sloan and Athian just looked over at me and nodded in acknowledgement. I was wondering where Krissy was and then suddenly I felt the edge of very sharp blade against my throat. "Morning" she said as she removed her arm from me and put her dagger back into its sheaf. She was always testing me, making sure I was prepared for anything. The morning had passed quite quickly and we had managed to help the gatherers and the hunters as-well as helping some of the others secure damaged fencing which had broken during a storm.

Return Of The Bloodstone

It came to midday and as we were all sat around the fire eating none of us mentioned the conversation that we had the night before. We all knew at some point that one of us had to speak about it. We knew that we had decided what we were going to do but we didn't know when we were going to do it. We had to leave the area in search of some greater support and then move on and face the threat of the ever growing evil.

Athian had just finished eating and to my surprise he was the one that decided to speak out "So when are we leaving then," as he said this I very nearly choked on my food. Luckily for me I managed to safely spit it out. "Mickel, seriously" "Sorry Krissy, I was shocked at what I heard." Even though we all had our own opinions we all acknowledged with each-other that we had to leave. Athian was right, It was more of a question as to when to leave.

Sloan informed us that we needed to search all the areas north of the wastelands before we even thought of heading back south. "Sloan, we don't have time to search the northern villages, what is it you are looking for," He understood my frustration and went on to tell us that he needs to find the village elders. He said "The elders have the knowledge of the world's history. Information that we will need in order to fight this battle and hopefully information on magical gemstones."

I decided to ask Sloan what other information it was that he needed. He looked at me with discontent before speaking "Mickel, I've read what I can from the book, I've understood all the spells and Incantation's that I can learn from it. While reading the book there was one page amongst them all that I read over and over again. This page explains how to draw evil out of something or some-one, this might be able to keep evil locked away. With what I seek we could use on Blaine, It's powers may be able to draw out the evil that inhabits your father's body, this could make him pure again." with Sloan saying this I completely relaxed myself and took a deep breath before speaking "What is it you need Sloan,?what do we need to find?" Sloan stood to his feet, raised his head and was looking out towards the distant fields and woodlands "A Bloodstone Mickel, we need to find a Bloodstone."

Sloan then spoke to Mickel "Mickel let me explain to you again. The Bloodstone's have been used for many generations. They have strong powers and are a positive energy stone. I have read from the book and with the right spell they can't only just heal someone but they can draw all evil out of people, objects or even places. They can cleanse a soul, this could possibly set your father free from the evil that currently resides in him."

Hearing this again with a clearer explanation a look of belief could be seen on Mickel's face. A belief that his father could still be saved. He stood up and looked at them all before speaking, "We leave in the morning."

They all went on through the rest of the day preparing

for what could be a long and dangerous journey ahead of them. They appointed some of the common folk duties to ensure they stayed as safe as they could be. They asked whom amongst them would volunteer to accompany them on their journey. They were all quiet, none of them were willing to leave the settlement and head out into the unknown. They felt safe where there were, they had found themselves a new home, somewhere away from the evil that was growing and spreading from the south. These people survived the chaos and destruction and were in no rush to see it again.

Night had arrived and they had everything they needed ready. Sloan was fully prepared mentally and tried his hardest to get Athian to the same mental state. Krissy prepared herself the best that she could, arming herself with her new dagger's and her new sword. She even had the forgers make her some new blades which were strapped around her elbows. They looked like giant silver claws growing out from the back of her arms. In order to efficiently use them she trained herself with new fighting techniques. With these and the other new weapons she had strapped to her body she looked dangerous. I certainly wouldn't want to face her as a foe in battle. With us all now knowing that there was a chance my father could be saved we had a new belief in ourselves. I was prepared to the best that I could be. I was eager to set off in search of the Bloodstone, I needed to save my father or what was left of him.

Return Of The Bloodstone

Chapter 2

Since Blaine had managed to survive the channelling room by subsiding in the body of Colias, the evil in the south had started to grow strong. He was exacting his hate and revenge upon the very world around him.

He had the city guards creating mass hysteria and fear amongst the citizens of paradise. Any who spoke out against him were imprisoned or beaten. The guards would completely plunder peoples homes and take anything they wanted. This was only the beginning, it was a message to all that would try to oppose him or refused to follow the new reign of power.

With the city holding many thousands of people, and most of them witnessing such events it led to many of them wanting to escape paradise. The walls of the city were now easier to climb and most people used this as a method to free themselves from the new horrors.

With his powers ever growing, It wasn't long before he had full control of paradise and all the trade coming into the city had soon ceased completely. People had stopped heading to the city for a so called better life.

They had heard of what was happening there and with the new look of the city and its surrounding areas it invoked fear into many. Any new travellers that entered the city were never free to do as they pleased. They were either forced to join his ever growing legion of evil or were tortured and killed.

It no longer looked like the mighty city that it once was. All the unique structures within it and around it had changed. Everything was now covered in large black roots. Roots rising from the deep ground, wrapping themselves around everything and crushing the glorious bricks. All the statues that were on the walls and the structures of the buildings were now covered from sight.

After the last day of sport any masters of light that remained in the city were banished, those that didn't leave the city had a choice to make, pledge themselves to Blaine or to be executed. Many refused to join his dark reign and tried to fight him with their magic, but he was too strong and in defeat they were publicly executed by either his dark magic or the city guards. He preferred execution as a form of punishment as he knew banishment doesn't remove the enemy, it just keeps it at a distance. With others witnessing him bestow this treatment upon the masters of light many found themselves pledging their loyalties to him.

With Davos and Delia being as faithful to Blaine as they were, he used his magic and invoked more power unto them. This made them both stronger than they had ever been before and they both ensured all in the city knew it. They would often just walk through the city and inflict pain and torture upon anyone they wanted. They would use their new obtained powers to do as they pleased. Some that were tortured or killed were done so by fire magic. This was a horrendous and a horrific way to die. They would use the magic fire by first causing a burning sensation in the feet and legs, this would then ignite and have them screaming in agony before completely self-combusting into a giant burning flame. Being tortured and killed in this manner left nothing but charred skeletal remains. Remains in this condition could been found scattered all throughout the city. They wouldn't allow them to be removed from where they lay, they kept them on show to impose more fear, some even thought that they did it for a decorative effect. This had made the city look more like an upturned graveyard rather than a place where people once lived.

Davos and Delia had the whole city guards at their command, along with any common folk that decided to follow them which formed a large army. Even with their stronger magic and their human army of guards Blaine wanted a stronger force to command. With the help Of Davos and Delia the three of them combined all their magic together allowing Blaine to open up a crevice. The crevice was either from hell itself or another realm but only Blaine knew the answer to this question.

He needed an area that was of a good size and flat in its centre. He decided the best place to open up such a vortex was in the arena of sport. It not longer looked like the mighty structure that it once was, it now looked more like a giant hollowed out tree trunk. All the giant roots that had grown around it were crushing the arena inwards, weakening the whole structure and any buildings that were attached to it.

With Davos and Delia concentrating hard Blaine was casting an incantation towards the clouds above them, They started to turn a dark black and no light could make it through them. They had managed to completely block out the sun from shining into the arena. From a distance outside of the city lightning could be seen striking down into it.   Although none of the common folk had witnessed what was happening in the arena, they knew it was something supernatural and evil. Many said that one day the ground just started to shake vigorously throughout the whole city. They could hear a large cracking sound and it felt like the very earth beneath them was being pulled apart. A dark black smoke then started to come from the arena, like there was a constant burning fire inside of it.

Some survivors that escaped the city had managed to tell others what it was that they saw coming from the arena or what was now in it. The reports were from the few that were brave enough to climb the black roots that covered the arena and watch what was happening inside. Only a few had managed to escape with their lives. Many inside the city wanted to see what was the cause was but with few returning they chose not to test their luck, however It didn't stop them from wondering what it was that was changing the world. Those that did witness what was happening escaped the city while they still could.

Word soon spread about what these survivors had seen In the arena. It was said that what was in the arena centre was a constant black smoke fluming from a hole with occasional bursts of fire. But this wasn't the only reason they decided to flee the city. Many say that they saw demons coming from the crevice. They said that they saw different types of demons. Some were in human form and others were in spiritual form moving freely in the air like a black mist. This invoked true fear into most of the common folk and led to thousands of them trying to flee the city. But not everyone left the city, some folk thought that they would be safer by keeping quiet and remaining loyal.

No-one was sure exactly what they were calling forth from the crevice, but when they arrived here in our world they could be seen to inflict death and punishment upon many. They were especially more aggressive when they were closer to the crevice. Should anyone get too close to it they would be taken by something dark, it was like a black mist, a shadow demon. The shadow demons had all different forms, some of them were the shape of man and others were in the shape of beasts or even a mixture of the two. The shadow demons weren't in physical form, they moved like a cloud through the darkness.

This crevice was a vortex, a vortex that Blaine had

opened and it's purpose was for one-thing only, it was to build an army. Blaine was building his army, his unholy army, his legion to bring death and destruction to our world. All the demons or creatures that came from the vortex were his to control.

Occasionally Blaine could be seen freely moving throughout his new city. He would never be seen alone though, now by his side and around him he appeared to have large demon hounds. They had a dark red complexion and large teeth protruding from their jaws. They didn't appear to have hair like normal hounds, they had what looked like burnt flesh, as if they had been partially skinned. They were big and muscular with large black eyes and had a constant drool that looked like blood dripping from their mouths. They followed Blaine every-where he went, never leaving his side. If Blaine didn't permit it and anyone got too close to him the hounds would pounce on them and tear them limb from limb. They would then devour what they could leaving nothing but chewed up remains and a blood soaked ground beneath them.

They didn't just do this to the common folk, they acted in the same manner against anyone, even the city guards if they got too close. After several city guards had been killed by the demon hounds they all quickly learnt to keep their distance from their master. The Demon hounds were his personal protection. His dark army was being formed with shadow demons, fire demons and other unholy creatures.

Return Of The Bloodstone

There was one of his dark creatures that was very muscular in physique, it had sharp teeth and long claws, they walked around just like people. They were always looking, always searching for anything they could kill and eat. Their skin was a greyish black colour with thick red veins. The most unique feature about them was that they had no eyes, they had eye sockets but no eyes, just a bright red lining along the edge of the eye sockets. They had small ear openings at the side of their heads and two small nostrils above a mouth which had hundreds of small razor sharp teeth. These beasts were what mostly made up the numbers in Blaine's unholy legion. They fully understood Blaine and obeyed his every command. They would move freely under the darkness that was above them. They would carry out any acts of aggression in unison. They moved together and acted as one. Although what had came out of the crevice was fearsome and dangerous none of them showed any sign of aggression towards Blaine. They were his to command and control, they were his unholy legion.

After the initial influx of unholy beasts coming from the vortex they appeared to of stopped coming into our world. Only a few of them every few days were now appearing. At the beginning it was a constant flow. Even though the demons entering our world had slowed down the vortex remained open, it remained open to bring into our world the dark black smoke which was filling the skies.

With Blaine now having these dark demons at his side

to command and the skies above the city in darkness it didn't take him long before he had dominated the city and the surrounding areas. Once Blaine had complete control of the city he started to prepare his plans for what was about to come. The skies above the city were so black that no light from the sun could shine through. A constant rumbling of thunder could be heard, never fading and never stopping. Strong bolts of lightning would strike the lands as the cloud inched its way outwards from the city and started to spread across the south.

He first started to spread this dark shroud of evil over the lands just outside of Paradise. The trees and plant life that once grew so well soon wilted to decay as they were deprived of the much needed light. The wild animal life that once roamed these lands either fled from or were slaughtered by the ever moving unholy legion.

Any Villages in this area were attacked and destroyed, villages being completely burnt to the ground. They left nothing behind but bodies and ash. Any people that weren't killed or didn't manage to escape soon found themselves at the mercy of the evil that was being forced upon them. They had but two options, join them or join the dead that lay scattered amongst the ashes.

Many villagers tried to defend their lands and their homes but the evil forces encroaching upon them were too fierce and brutal. Not only did they have to face Davos and Delia's magic but they also had to face their brutal city guards and any of the unholy demons that were moving behind them. The cloud filling the skies moved slowly and it took many months for the surrounding areas of Paradise to be covered in darkness. The corpses that lay in the city graveyard were summoned from their resting places and roamed the lands freely. They had no knowing of life or death and just wandered the lands. For the common folk the mere sight of seeing rotting corpses and skeletal remains walking the lands put fear into most that looked upon them.

Davos and Delia were tasked with overseeing the forced change of the lands. They needed to ensure that they used loyal men and strong city guards to start the destruction of the villages and the onslaught of the villagers that lay before them.

As the area became enshrouded in darkness only then could the legion of Blaine's unholy army move forward. Moving from area to area while remaining in the darkness. Occasionally some of the demons would go into a killing frenzy and chase down anything that was running from them. They would completely lose their sense of having to stay in the dark, and as they hunted down their victims they would move into areas that were still under sunlight. This was their only mistake, this highlighted a weakness amongst them. By running into the sunlight it showed that they could be hurt, but more than than that is showed that they could be killed. Although they could lose a fight against good warriors, sunlight was the easiest method to inflict pain upon them or kill them. Should they ever get trapped in sunlight their skin would blister and burn, they would scream a horrible high pitch cry of agony before eventually turning to dust.

The dark beings needed the dark to survive, with sunlight being the main thing to stop them, they had to move with the darkness. The demons that all the common folk feared the most were the fire demons. They didn't die in the sunlight, it only appeared to hurt them and fire had no effect upon them. They would absorb heat from fire and appeared to get stronger from it, their weakness was still to be found. While the sunlight was slowly being stripped away from the world all the demons had to wait before they could cause death and destruction. This is the reason why Blaine was filling the skies with an evil black shroud. The further that the lands fell under darkness the further that his unholy demons could move out into the world.

After an area of land had fallen into the shadows of the dark skies it would soon fall to the demons. They would take control of the dark lands ensuring that nothing survived. Once under full control of an area the demons would lay in the dark and wait to move forward until it was safe for them to do so. They would have to wait for the dark clouds above them to claim more land before they could bring more mayhem. They would sometimes lay in the darkness for weeks, just waiting for the chance to move forward again to destroy, kill and feed.

Return Of The Bloodstone

Even though the sunlight would prevent them from moving forward they would however move freely through the night. They would travel out as far as they could under the natural darkness. Moving into lands that had yet to be taken under control.

Blaine's legion lost a lot of demons to sunlight or by getting trapped in fire. They may be big and viscous but their lust and hunger to bring death and chaos would sometimes force them too far out from the unnatural darkness. Not knowing completely how far out they were a new day would dawn and as with each new day comes a new sun rise. Any demons not under the safety of the unnatural darkness were soon dust in the wind.

Blaine wasn't pleased to be losing many of his demons and often showed this with his rage and anger. He had to continuously ensure the vortex stayed open. This was currently the only way that he could summon more demons and unholy creatures into our world, it was also the source of the evil black shroud that was forming his new world. Blaine could control most of what was happening from the temple. He would sit in his throne constantly casting incantations and spells to ensure the world was changing to how he wanted it. If anywhere currently under darkness and his control would start to to slip from his grasp then he would focus his attention there. The hardest part of his plan was preventing the sunlight from breaking through the dark clouds. On occasions certain areas were affected by sunlight breaking through the clouds, this prevented his legion from moving through those parts of land. He needed complete focus and complete control of what he was doing. Without the dark shroud in the skies the ground below wouldn't decay and rot. He needed every area to be dark and dead.

Approximately nine months had passed since Blaine's return and he had managed to spread darkness across the lands and woods to just south of the swamp. He knew that if he wanted complete control then he would had to have at least half of this world. He needed the swamps and the wastelands to fall to his evil legion, the whole of his world would then soon be his.

The deadly winds of the wastelands and the dead army that moves within them are only ever present at night. As with the demons, sunlight has the same effect on the dead that walk amongst the wasteland. Blaine knew that if he could convert the wastelands into complete darkness then he could add this evil to his unholy army.

Armies and hunters from the north had heard of what evil was moving towards them from the south. Many village elders from the Argian valley had gathered and discussed what they were to do with the evil that was coming their way. They voted and decided to form an army, they sent a small part of this army south to see exactly what it was that was heading their way. A thousand hunters from many tribes were said to of been formed and sent on this task. The Journey through the wastelands and swamps was going to be a dangerous one, but they knew it had to be done. As committed as these men were they had to see exactly what it was they needed to prepare for. Most of these men didn't manage to return to the Argian Valley, If the wastelands didn't take them, then the swamp creatures did.

It was said that hundreds of them heading south never even made it to the wastelands. As they marched south from the Argian Valley they could see the dark black skies far in the distance, they could hear its thunder and see the lightning strikes constantly hitting the lands. This led to many of them deserting partway through the wastelands and quickly attempting to make their way back north. Many that made it through the wastelands decided not to travel any further, not even wanting to step foot into the swamps. They thought that it was a safer risk to head back north to the elders and report what they had seen without any confrontation. Even knowing that the wastelands had many dangers, they would rather face those risks rather than something they didn't understand. Many had decided to abandon their given quest and not many of them made it back to the valley. Travelling through the heat of the wastelands in the day was bad enough but trying to travel through them at night was worse. Many of them fell victim to it's evil that roam there. Those that did manage to make it back safely were able to report to the elders what they had saw. They reported that an evil could be seen in the distance and fear could be felt to be coming from all who saw it. They told the elders how the south was completely in blackness and how the land and life down there was dead or dying. Even though the evil hadn't yet managed to reach the swamp they all knew that they had to prepare, they had to prepare for a fight, they had to prepare for survival. The elders had a name for what they were preparing for, they called it death.

Chapter 3

The morning had soon arrived, Sloan, Athian and Krissy were all prepared and ready to go, they were just waiting on me. I wasn't being hesitant but I had to give the people staying behind clear instructions. They needed to know what to do should anything hostile threaten them. Using the skills and knowledge gained since they had been here they knew that fire was the best means of delaying or stalling an enemy. Once I was satisfied that they fully understood their instruction to protect the people and the book I gathered everything I needed and then went and met up with the others.

We all decided together that we should leave the camp in the most likely direction that we would find people, so we started our journey heading east, following the best easterly trail that we could find. I wasn't sure if this was the right direction or not, but we had to take the risk. We kept following any paths that we felt and looked likely to be the safest ones. Sloan needed us to find any Argian settlements that had elders within them. He needed to know where he could find any remaining Bloodstone's and he was hoping that the elders had the answers to this questions.

As for looking for Argian villages, the only places that I knew of were close to my home village, and we were a good distance from them. I knew that there were more villages around but I wasn't sure where they were or if they had any elders in them or not. The elders kept our worlds history alive, passing any knowledge onto those who were next in-line to succeed them, hoping that what they knew would one day be understood if it was ever needed.

We must of walked for several hours and we hadn't met a single person, but we didn't let this stop us from searching, it felt good to get out of the settlement. Eventually we came to an area that looked like it was recently used as a camp site, we could clearly see a built up resting area around a burnt out fire. This was a sign to us that people had been here, we took this as a good sign. From this area if we looked to the south we could see the dark black sky in the horizon. It was past the wastelands and the swamp but yet it seemed to be closer to us than what it was. It was moving northwards slowly, but it was surely coming our way. We tried our best not to focus on it, but with it now being closer and as large as what it was we couldn't stop turning our heads to gaze upon it, well more like to stare at it. "I don't like the look it Mickel." "Don't worry Athian, it's still a good distance from us."

Return Of The Bloodstone

We used the camp-site that we had found to rest and while we were here we searched the area for any clues we could find as to who was here before us. We tried to find clues as to which direction that they had left the camp-site in. Sloan was the best at tracking and he spent quite a while searching the whole area "Some of the tracks led south towards the wastelands and the other tracks came into the camp-site from the north, It's not just a southward march as there are other tracks that leave the camp-site returning to the north." Krissy and I kept searching the ground for any dropped items, we weren't looking for anything specific, we were just looking for items that might help us.

Although Sloan had found tracks he still didn't know exactly which direction was the best one to take. He started to us a magic incantation and told Athian to gather some ashes from the camp fire. Athian gathered as many ashes as he could and returned to Sloan with them. "Athian, when I tell you to, you must throw the ashes into the wind swirl that I create." The spell that Sloan was casting required him to move his hands in a circular motion, as he was doing this a bright blue light started to appear before him. The light then started to swirl around like a miniature whirlwind. It was spinning faster and faster, creating a small strong wind vortex pulling anything near it towards it's centre. Krissy and I kept our distance and just watched on, we weren't sure exactly what was happening but we both knew that Sloan had became strong and efficient with his magic so we left him to undertake any incantations as he needed to. The whirlwind was now spinning so fast that it was difficult to ignore and to not focus on it, being very curious as to what he was doing we moved ourselves closer. "Now Athian, throw the ashes into the vortex." Athian opened both hands and released the cold dark ash in to the spinning vortex whirlwind. At first it didn't look like anything was happening, but then the light and the ash combined themselves and were spinning together. Sloan kept speaking the incantation and we then noticed that the ash had separated itself from the vortex light. It was taking a shape of it's own, It was forming a line, binding itself together stretching itself out away from the spinning vortex that Sloan had created.

Sloan suddenly stopped speaking the incantation and the light instantly disappeared. As he did this the ash dropped to the ground as a solid item. We were expecting to fall apart back to it's original shape but it didn't, it stayed solid and as as straight as an arrow. As it hit the ground it appeared to form what looked like a marker, a directional marker. It was showing us which way it was that we had to go. It wasn't just giving us a direction, it gave us the direction that the previous people headed off in. Athian dusted of his hands and Sloan then spoke to us all "this is the direction that we must go." I looked at Sloan before asking "north, are you sure we need to go north." "Yes." replied Sloan. "But that's not the direction that we should be heading." "I told you Mickel, we need to find a Bloodstone, without a Bloodstone we can't continue on this journey." I looked at him in dismay and knew that he was correct. Krissy could see from my reaction that I was slightly annoyed so she then decided to speak, hoping to change the atmosphere amongst us. "So we head north then, come one boys, what are you waiting for."

We stopped searching the area for any dropped items and decided to listen to Sloan and agreed that north would be the direction we follow. I knew that if we kept heading in a north or north-easterly direction then sooner or later we would arrive back in my village. I hadn't been at the village since Athian and myself left there over a year ago. How could we return to tell my people that an evil is coming there way and that it was all my fault.

We didn't stay in the camp site for any longer than what we needed to. we only stayed long enough to have a little rest before we again set off on our travels. I knew several of the villages in the far north so if we could find one that I could recognise it would make it easier for us to know where we were. We must of walked for several more hours before we came across the first village. After not walking this far for a while my feet started to really ache and it wasn't just me feeling this way. So we took advantage of any opportunity to rest.

As we approached the village many of the villagers quickly ran from us and hid from sight. We may of possibly startled them and they could of thought that we were going to be hostile. Sloan and Athian didn't look so hostile but with Krissy being armed to her teeth it may of given off a different impression. I could imagine that they might of felt the same way about my appearance. I was unable to hide my sword and shield from sight, they were too large to keep hidden so they were always clearly on show, anyway I didn't want to hide them. I wanted them to be readily available and quick to hand should I ever require them.

As we walked further into the village we all heard a noise coming from behind us. The hunters of this village had quickly gathered and were soon upon us. Many of them had spears or their hunting bows all drawn back and all of which were pointing directly at us. "Please, there is no need for hostility, I am Mickel from the northern village. We are seeking your village elder." We could see that they were scared and they were a bit reluctant to lower their weapons. One of the hunters then appeared with and elderly man and it was only then that they lowered their weapons. "What do you want?" asked the elderly man. "Are you the village elder? we need to seek his guidance." The man turned from us and walked away without saying a word. We were thinking that this village wasn't one we needed and we were going to get little help from the people here. The elderly man that was walking away from us suddenly stopped, turned his head and was looking back at us "Follow me" He led us to a hut that was on the far side of the village. We followed him keeping as close together as we could, while we were following him the hunters were following us, only ever keeping a few steps behind us.

As we walked further through the village we noticed women and children had started to appear from their homes. The children seemed happy to see us, they were running out to greet us, they stayed close to us and plenty of them kept trying to touch our weapons. We didn't want any of them to get hurt so we had to encourage the women to move them away from us.

We had followed the old man a good distance and he soon walked into a hut, as he entered he told us to wait outside. We stood waiting outside the hut for a while before he eventually reappeared. He asked for the holder to step forth and enter the hut. We all looked at each in confusion. "The holder? The holder of what?" asked Athian "Only the holder may enter the hut." As none of us were sure what he meant I decided that we needed more clarification and asked him a question "What do you mean only the holder? Only the holder of what?" The elderly man didn't say another word, he simply just walked away from us and went back about his business.

I was thinking that it didn't matter who entered the hut as-long as one of us entered. Any one of us could have been the holder, we still didn't know what it was that one of us was meant to be the holder of. We all spoke to each-other and decided that one of us had to enter, one of us would have to explain what it is that we are looking for. I was the first to try, I walked towards the entrance door of the hut as I got closer to it I started to feel a pounding in my head and I struggled to breathe. I didn't know what was happening to me. I was in an unbearable pain and I couldn't enter the hut, it felt like my head was in a vice, slowly but surely being pressed inwards and it wasn't just my head, it felt like my chest was being crushed also. Krissy was the first to notice what was happening to me and she quickly pulled me away from the entrance of the hut. As I got further back from the entrance the painful sensations that I was feeling soon faded away. Athian then walked towards the hut's entrance "Let me try." As he approached the door the same thing started to happen to him. Only for Athian it appeared to be worse, he collapsed to the ground holding his head and was barely able to breathe. Sloan and I quickly pulled him away from the hut and as with myself the pain that was being inflicted upon him faded away. We weren't sure what was happening, it didn't seem right. Sloan stood staring at us and then he stared at the hut before speaking "The hut is enchanted" he then walked towards the entrance and was expecting the same thing to happen, but he felt nothing. He continued to walk forward and placed his hand upon the door. As he did this there was a brief flash of light and Sloan then pushed the door open. He put one foot inside the hut and he still wasn't affected by any head or chest pains. He was the holder, Sloan was the one that the elders were willing to speak with.

Sloan had now completely entered the hut while we waited outside. We were constantly being watched by the village hunters. They didn't fully trust us and we could still see fear in their eyes. They didn't understand who we were or why we were here.

While Sloan was entering the hut we managed to catch a quick glimpse of what was inside. We couldn't see any people but we were able to see a small fire which was burning in the middle of the room, next to the fire there was a chopped log and beside that there appeared to be dagger, a strange looking dagger which looked like it was made from bone rather than steel. It was in a wooden bowl and alongside it was what looked like a dirty yellow stagnant water. It didn't look like normal water, it had steam or smoke rising from it, it looked like it had been taken from a marsh.

Sloan approached the fire and knew exactly what to do, he knelt down before it. He picked up the knife in one hand and the dirty water in the other. He quickly drank the drink but he didn't swallow all of it. He was keeping some of it in his mouth. After drinking the filthy water he then opened the palm of his free hand and held it out above the bowl. He placed the bone blade onto his open palm and slid the blade across it, slicing deep enough to cause an open wound and draw blood. He then clenched his hand to form a fist and held it over the bowl. Blood dripped freely from his hand, dripping down into the bowl, drop after drop, once there was enough blood in the bowl he then spat the remaining water from his mouth into it. As the water mixed with his blood it started to swirl. A red smoke then started to rise from the bowl. Sloan suddenly felt himself going into a sleep like trance. His eyes rolled backward into his skull revealing just the whites of his eyes. Although he was in a trance he sat completely upright and as he did this an image of a man appeared from the smoke. The man looked very old, as if he was one from ancient times and was no longer with us in this world. Although Sloan was in a trance he still had all of his senses, he could see the man before him but couldn't tell if he was of spiritual or physical form. Sloan then heard a slow ancient voice speaking to him "What is it you seek?" Sloan replied without knowing "We need to find a Bloodstone, can you help us?" The ancient voice once again spoke to Sloan "The Bloodstone is lost, protected from all who try to seek it. why do you need to seek what might end in disaster?" Again without knowing it he replied to the man by explaining all to him what had happened over the last year and what was currently happening to the world. "I need knowledge, I need to find the Bloodstone and the knowledge on how to stop this evil that is now present in our world. Will you help me?"

With Sloan unknowingly giving this man all the information he could, he was hoping to have a response back, but it never came. But what did happen was that Sloan started to shake and convulse, while he was in this condition he started to have visions, visions of the world's history, he was seeing ancient battles between the dark masters and the masters of light. He saw death and destruction being caused by magic and mythical beasts. His visions were clear to him, he saw common folk being slaughtered and devoured by demonic monsters, villages were being burnt to the ground. He could see an image of a man, he couldn't make out the man's face but this man was standing alongside the masters of light and he was fighting against the unholy armies.

The visions soon changed from death and destruction and he was then seeing the common folk amongst the masters of light. They were working together, using magical spells and physical tools to destroy what appeared to be gemstones. He then saw different gemstones all gathered together. They were the ones that weren't destroyed, they were being locked away into different types of chests. They were then scattered throughout the world. One of these gemstones that was being locked away and hidden within the world was the Bloodstone. It was being put inside a cast Iron chest. The chest was marked with what appeared to be ancient writing and magical glyphs. It was then sealed with an Iron chain and loaded on to a ship. The visions that Sloan was seeing suddenly stopped, and as they disappeared from his mind he fell to floor of the hut. He remained there in a sleep like state for several minutes before regaining consciousness. As he stood to his feet he looked around the room for the man that he had been talking to but there was no-one there, he was alone.

Sloan eventually came out of the hut and was looking a little paler than his usual complexion. He looked around the area and was pleased to see that the village hunters had left us alone. As I saw Sloan leaving the hut I stood to my feet and asked him what was said to him? "There was no-one there Mickel, the hut was empty." "No one there! how could there of been no one there? We could hear you talking Sloan, we could hear someone else talking to you. What was said Sloan? don't hide this from us."

In regards to what was said to Sloan in the hut, he told Mickel nothing. All he said was that they would find no more help here and that we needed to continue our search. Athian decided to ask him where we were going to next. Sloan quietly replied "Somewhere with a boat, we will need a boat to find what we seek,"

We decided that now was the time to leave the village and continue on our search for other elders. During our journey north through the valley lands Sloan eventually decided to speak to us about what had happened in the hut. He mentioned all the visions that he had seen and the message that these visions were showing unto him. "The Bloodstone was locked away and sent somewhere on a ship. I don't know where, but it was sent out to sea." I listened clearly to what Sloan was telling us and I kept thinking to myself that if the Bloodstone was sent out to sea, then why continue on our journey looking for other elders? I decided to ask him a question in which I was hoping to get the response I wanted. "Sloan, what are we looking for from other elders?" He simply replied "More answers Mickel, more answers to more questions."

The day had started to come to an end and as the sun

was starting to set we could see the darkness from the south merging with the natural darkness of night. We soon found ourselves setting up camp in the middle of the Argian valley. We quickly gathered as much wood as we could and encircled ourselves with a wall of fire. Not knowing how much of the land was crawling with dark and evil creatures, we had to ensure that we stayed as safe as we possibly could.

Although we could see the darkness moving up from the south and we could still slightly hear the rumbling of thunder, we weren't quite sure how far north the evil had travelled. The whole of the north was in a race against time, should the swamp fall into a permanent darkness then the wastelands wouldn't be far behind. The only way that man could travel through the wastelands with minimal danger was during the day, and if they fell into complete darkness then the Argian valley and the wolf mountains would soon be over run by Blaine's unholy legion.

We made sure that the camp fires were kept lit all through the night. If any of them burnt too low then Sloan would us his magic to try to reignite them. Sloan couldn't keep them burning with magic for long periods as it drained strength from him. Krissy sat most the of night awake, just staring out in to the darkness. Waiting in anticipation that something was going to make its way to us. She was prepared for a fight. She kept watch over us, waiting to put a dagger or sword into anything that wished us harm. She has been away from her home and duties for over a year now but she still tries her best to keep her fighting spirit alive. If Sloan wasn't able to keep the fires burning by magic then we ensured that we all took turns in keeping them lit with wood.

While three of us slept the other one was always awake, keeping a watch over us and the fires. Over the year that had passed we had all became very good friends, we understood each other, we relied on each other. If the truth were told, we felt more like a family rather than friends, a lot can happen in a year, bonds can be made and bonds can be broken. We stayed together, we lived together and we were bound to each-other.

The night seemed to pass by quite quickly and as the sun rose in the horizon we were relieved to see that the lands behind us were still touched by sunlight. It was an amazing sight to see the world come to life as the sunlight and its warm touch reached the ground. The trees would shine a bright green, the rivers would glisten with a bright white shine as they freely flowed and any flowers would open up and absorb as much sunlight as they could. Small rodents would even come out of their burrows and start to gather what food they could find. It felt strange knowing that all this would come to an end if we couldn't stop the evil that was growing and heading this way.

As morning was now with us I quickly got to my feet "come on then, let's get going, we don't have much time," to which Athian responded "What with no breakfast," "yes

Athian, with no breakfast, I'm sure you will be able to eat more than your fill once we get to the next village." "Eat more than my fill, come on then, what are we waiting for." At hearing this conversation between Athian and myself Sloan started to laugh and was quick to respond "If I knew that was the best method to get him to do anything I would of used it six months ago." We then all started to laugh loudly as one, even knowing with the dangers ahead of us and the world changing, laughing together kept us close.

We left the camp and started to head north, we were looking for the next village, hopefully a village with more elders and ones that could answer Sloan's questions. I kept thinking to myself that it was strange that the old man in the previous village openly brought us to the hut. Maybe we got lucky, or maybe they were expecting us. Either way I didn't let it play on my mind too much. All I knew was that if there was a Bloodstone out there, then we were the ones that had to find it.

Athian and myself started to recognise where we were. This area of the Argian valley is a quite well known area to most northerners. There are plenty of small villages in this area but none of them had any elders residing within them. Most of the elders reside in the larger villages. Through the day we passed through many small villages and all of them had no advice or help that they were able to offer us.

We eventually came to a larger village, and I recognised

this one well, this was the main hunters village. It didn't just contain most of the northern hunter's, but it contained most of the northern fighters also. It's only a four to five hour walk from my home village. This village surely had an elder or more. As we started to walk through the village we noticed that there we no people, there was no-one out of their homes, no-one on the market stalls and no-one was selling trade. It didn't feel right, something here was wrong. Krissy had noticed this also and took out her daggers sensing that something was going to happen "Something here isn't right Mickel, this is no trading village," Sloan felt this also and told Athian to stand and stay behind him. We all walked cautiously through the village, being as careful as we could. That's when I heard a noise, it was a whistling noise that was coming at us through the air. Just as I turned to see what it was Krissy pulled me to ground. As she did this an arrow flew past my head and sunk deep into a wooden crate which was conveniently placed at the front of a hut. It was at this point we started to hear people shouting out loudly. Whoever it was shouting out they weren't just being vocal, they launched many arrows towards us.

I quickly pulled up my shield to give Krissy and myself protection. I could hear the arrows hitting my shield hard. Luckily for me it had been forged with good solid minerals and most of the arrows were being deflected away. We managed to move towards a wall of crates and logs, we kept ourselves low behind them to shield us from any potential harm. The arrows were coming at us too quickly for us to be able to safely move away. We could hear them piercing into the crates and we could see splinters of wood flying through the air in all directions.

Sloan had told us to stay still and not to move. We did exactly as he said and made sure that we were under full cover. Athian was trying to call up a spell, he wanted to put a magical shield around us but he failed in his attempt. We could hear a voice shouting from one the of houses "Die demons, return to where you belong."

Hearing this I then shouted out "Stop please stop, we are not here to hurt you," they didn't seem to listen to me as more arrows were launched through the air in our direction. I decided to try again "Stop, we beg of you, I am Mickel, son of Colias from the northern town on the seas." This time It appeared to of worked. The arrows being shot towards us started to reduce before then stopping completely. Once the danger being launched towards us had stopped, people started to appear from the surrounding trees, the tops of huts and from behind the crates that were opposite us.

I then heard a voice call my name "Mickel, son of Colias," "yes it is I" "Come out and show yourselves, be sure that you have no weapons in your hands." Krissy didn't want to put her daggers away, she wanted to go out and fight. I had to explain to her that she couldn't fight these people. "These are mine and Athian's people Krissy, we can't hurt them." She wasn't happy with the decision but she understood.

We all put our weapons away and walked out from behind the now destroyed fruit crates. Amongst the men and women that were stood in front of us I recognised a face, a regular face from our village. It was our village elder. He instantly recognised Athian and myself and told his fighters that it was okay and to go back about their tasks.

He walked towards us and stopped directly in front of me. He looked over us each individually and then told us that we had come at the right time. "The right time!" I asked "Yes, the right time, we have heard of the evil that is growing in the south. We are preparing for what may come our way. We are building an army, an army to fight this evil that is on the rise." I couldn't believe what I was hearing. The elders were always against violence and now they were encouraging it by training and developing common folk into fighters. "These people are not fighters, you don't know what's coming." The elder looked at me again before speaking "Walk with me Mickel."

After walking away with him I had to tell him that we were not here to join his army, but we were in search of a Bloodstone. He didn't raise his head once, he just kept walking forward and asked me one thing "Colias, is he dead?," I told him that he wasn't dead but that he had an evil inside of him, that the evil has taken control of his body and had trapped his soul away. The soul of my father is lost with-in himself and the one soul in control was that of Blaine. When I mentioned that name he stopped walking and asked me one question, "Are you sure it is the soul of Blaine?" With a quiet tone in my voice and a slight nod of my head I confirmed that it was.

He then took us all into a hut where there were several other elders that were all sat around an open fire. They were all staring directly in to its centre. The elder told us to sit and then asked us how they could help. We explained to them about Sloan's vision and that we needed to know if there was any knowledge passed on through the generations on lost gemstones. we needed to know where the Bloodstone was hidden. He looked at us all and told us to stay in the hut, "rest and eat, I will return shortly." We decided to take him up on his offer and as we all sat down all the elders stood up and left the hut. One by one they left without speaking a word, not even looking at us. Where they all went to we didn't know.

It had been a long day, so we made sure that we rested and had some food. It was nice to have a good meal here. On the fire was a rabbit stew simmering away and Athian was eating as much of it as he could. "Told you that you would eat more than your fill."

A few hours had passed before the elder eventually came back in to the hut. We had all finished eating and managed to have a little rest. He came and sat amongst us. You have a quest that you must complete, to complete this quest you will need a boat." This confirmed

Sloan's vision, we each clearly remembered that Sloan had told us the same thing.

Chapter 4

The darkness from the south was moving a little further north everyday. Davos and Delia didn't need to have the evil cloud above them in order to cause havoc and chaos. All the lands now south of the swamp were under the dark reign of Blaine. His legion were now part way through dominating the swamp lands. What lived in the swamplands were not common folk, but what lived there was different types of beasts and creatures. These had managed to evolve in order to live and survive in such conditions. When the city guards attempted to take control of the swamp they were not expecting such a resilient defence and fight. Many city guards and loyal common folk to Blaine were killed while trying to clear out the life forms that lived here. They needed the cloud to move further forward. They needed it to be over the swamps so the demons could clear this area with little haste and much more ease.

With the elder returning to the hut from where he went and telling Mickel and the others that they needed a boat they all knew that their journey was far from over. They also knew that all the elders were here in this village, a few elders wouldn't of been able to make this decision on their own. They were here, we weren't sure where in the village, but they were all here together.

With all the elders of the northern villages here together it meant that something was happening. Something was happening that they all needed to agree upon. What were they all doing together? My father always told me that they would never take a risk of them all being together in one place at the same time.

I decided to ask "Why are all the elders here together" I got a look of disappointment from our village elder before he spoke "You know not to question an elder. But I must tell you, we are here to prevent what is happening to the world. We have gathered all the local hunters to form an army and for us to study the ancient scribes together."

The Ancient scribes contained generations of knowledge on magic, evil or good and how to return it to the world or defeat it. They had taken their time in gathering the elders so they would be ready for those who require the knowledge to prevent the change of the world. That time appears to be now. I remember talk of the ancient scribes yet I don't ever remember seeing one or others speaking of what they looked like.

Our village elder then decided to speak to us more about the scribes. "A thousand years ago the scribes were separated amongst many different parts of the world. At a time when magic was thought to of been fading from the world. They were granted to the ancient elders and these were all hidden from sight. Each scribe is kept secret and safe from sight of all others"

Amongst the scribes that they had managed to collectively bring together they obtained some vital information. Information on the magical gemstones that were hidden in the world, one of these gemstones that was hidden, was the Bloodstone. All they knew on it's location was that the Bloodstone was sent to sea. It was said that it was sent to a place where it would not be retrieved easily. Locked away and taken by nature to be kept protected until a time that it would be needed once again.

With Mickel and Athian both knowing the one elder they were able to speak to him freely. They told him that they knew where there was a boat, but they needed to know exactly where to go once they were on it. The elder looked at them both intently and told them to listen very carefully as he would only say it once "you need to enter the northern seas and travel east. Travel east until the you no longer have control and let the winds guide you. they will take you to your destination. Do not fight against nature, if you fight against nature then you will never find what you seek. When you are no longer able to go forward you must go down, but beware, what lies in the deep protects and defends what it has been offered or what it has taken. You must search for and find the Bloodstone. You will have one chance to return it to the world. Fail here and the growing darkness will devour all in it's path."

We all sat listening very carefully, making sure that we understood what was being told to us. "Mickel you will have a decision to make. But only you can make this decision, you cannot be the holder, but the decision must be yours and yours alone. Now go from here, we are finished, we can help you no more."

As the elder left the hut Athian looked across at Krissy and said "well that was intense," With a roll of her eyes and a slight nod of her head Krissy was in agreement. Sloan then stood up and told the others "prepare to leave, we have a boat to find." Mickel looked at Sloan and smiled before speaking, "don't worry about that, I know where there's a perfectly god boat," Athian jumped to his feet and blurted out "Yes, time to go home." It was just past midday and they still had several hours of daylight left. They were given horses by the village leader to ensure that they could get to the northern sea village quickly and hopefully with some daylight left to spare. They all straddled their horses and started to head north. Athian and Mickel led the way as they knew exactly where they were going.

Krissy was riding alongside Sloan watching the others in front. She then looked over to him and said "Are they racing each other," "I believe they are Krissy, I believe they are." Krissy wasn't going to let them have all the fun, so with a hard tap on her horses thigh she raced off ahead of Sloan. It didn't take her long before she was soon riding alongside them both. Mickel and Athian couldn't believe what they were seeing. They tried to get their horses to go faster but with Krissy being small and light they had no chance of catching up with her.

It wasn't long before they could see the village ahead of them. It was at this point they brought their horses to a slow walking pace, allowing them to recover and a chance for Sloan to catch up.

They rode the horses into the village as slowly and as quietly as they could. They didn't want to cause a panic amongst any villagers that saw them. They got to Mickel's home and stopped just behind it. They all made sure that they kept the horses out of sight. We dismounted our horses and secured them to a tree. As I was securing my horse I looked back and saw that Athian had stayed on his. I told him to come down and to come into the house. He didn't move from where he sat, he was high above us looking down at me. I could see the look in his eyes, he didn't want to come down from his horse, not here anyway, he wanted to go home. For over a year now all he had wanted to do was to go home, and now that he was back he needed to do something, he needed to see his mother. Knowing exactly what he wanted, I just told him "we leave at first light."

Athian slowly headed off down the path towards his house. Once arriving at his home he dismounted his horse and walked towards the door. As he reached the door he gave it a little knock. He got no response so he decided to knock again, only this time a little harder "knock knock knock" He still heard nothing, as he was about to knock the door for a third time he heard shuffling coming from inside his house. He then saw the door handle slowly start to turn and as the door opened he looked up and saw that he was looking into his mothers eyes. "Hello mother" he said. She looked at him not saying a word, she put out her hand and lightly brushed his cheek before wrapping her arms around him. She was holding him so tightly that he could barely breathe. As she removed her arms from around him she leaned forward and kissed him on his forehead. She then took him by the hand and guided him into the house closing the door behind them. She led him across the main room and sat him down in his chair.

She was pleased to see him, the tears kept rolling down her cheeks. She wiped them away as often as she could, she looked at Athian with a little smile upon her face and asked "are you hungry son?" "Starving mother, I'm always hungry." She started to prepare him some food and placed it on the table where he was sat. "Where have you been, I've been so worried, I thought you were dead."

Athian started to tell his mother about everything that they had been through over the last year. He told her about his journey down south and all that they had encountered along the way. He explained to her that Paradise City was real, but it wasn't a good place and all should avoid it.

Return Of The Bloodstone

Every time his mother tried to speak to him he would speak over her voice. Speaking louder both with excitement and fear in his tone. They continued to sit together throughout the evening. Eventually she asked "Where is Mickel?" "He's home mother, he's fine" "Is Colias with him" "No mother, we fear that Colias is gone." She didn't say much more, she just sat holding his hand listening to his story.

Back at Mickel's house they had quickly managed to relax. "I'm so looking forward to sleeping in my bed again" Sloan and Krissy were both trying to relax the best that they could. As this area was new to them they still had doubt of trusting new people and new surroundings. They both tried not to let it bother them too much as they knew they would soon be leaving and they fully trusted Mickel.

Sloan was sat in Colias's chair and was closing his eyes every moment he could. Krissy was sat by the fire playing with a dagger. She had a unique skill where she could lose grip of the handle and roll the blade around her hand. It would move swiftly spinning around her hand before stopping on top of it. She tried to teach me this trick but I kept nicking my fingers and palm with the blade, eventually after many failed attempts and many cuts I decided to give up on learning that skill.

Before settling off to sleep I had to explain to them that under no circumstances must they go through the village. The villagers here use to be acceptable of new people but are now probably nervous of strangers, especially ones that look like they are ready for battle. They didn't have many problems with outsiders from the village, but that was before we left and with what's happening in the world I'm sure that they would now be weary of new people. Several hours had passed and we managed to get warm and fill our stomachs once again. The food that was left in the house was no good so we had to use some of our provisions. We were now all ready for a good sleep. Sloan was comfortable in my father's chair so he decided to stay there. Krissy would of preferred to of slept somewhere with less comfort like outside but she eventually agreed to stay in the house and rested in my fathers room. I slept in my room, it was nice to lay in the comfort of my bed once again.

It was late in the night and we were all in a deep sleep when suddenly we were woken by a loud banging on the door. "Bang Bang Bang" with the shock of the unexpected noise I fell out of my bed and hit the floor hard. I quickly got to my feet and ran to the door to see what was happening.

I could see Sloan stood in the middle of the room preparing to cast a spell at whomever it was knocking the door. I looked back up the stairs and I could see Krissy stood there with a dagger in her hand, she was ready and prepared for a fight. "Who is it, who's there?" "Open the door Mickel" it was Athian. I quickly opened the door and pulled him inside. "What is it, what's wrong" he could barely speak, he was out of breath and had sweat dripping down from his forehead. "We have to go Mickel, we have to go now before it's too late."

None of us knew exactly what he was shouting about "What do you mean we have to go?" Athian stood looking at everyone and was trying his best to steady his breathing. "I was with my mother" exhaling quickly and then pausing before speaking again "I told her of our journey south, I told her about what we had been through and what was coming this way" I wasn't too sure why this would have him running from his house and knocking heavily on my door before telling us that we needed to leave. "This is no reason to leave, I'm sure your mother thinks you are exaggerating the story." "She didn't believe me Mickel, she didn't believe what I was telling her. After we sat for a while and I told her it all over again I could still see that she didn't believe me." We were all quiet just looking at him feeling sad for him. Just as we thought he had finished speaking he spoke again "She didn't believe me Mickel, so I showed her." I looked at him with confusion in my eyes "what have you done Athian?, what did you show her?" "Magic, I showed her a few of the little spells I had learnt." they couldn't believe what they were hearing. Sloan looked at Athian and we could all see the fury in his facial expression "What have I told you, common folk fear it, they don't understand it."

They quickly gathered up all their belongings and to avoid being seen they left the house by the rear entrance. As Sloan and Krissy didn't know the village or the way down to the boats they decided to follow Mickel.

They moved quietly around the outside of the house and into the shadows, moving in the bushes that bordered the path. They could hear talking coming from the village and as they looked across the path they could see the villagers gathering together. They then heard raised voices and anger within them.

Most of them had torches lit and others had farming tools or knives. They left the village centre and started to walk towards Mickel's house. With the villagers walking up the path towards the house we could see that it was a woman that was leading them, it was Athian's mother. In the shadows of the night we stood as quietly as we could to avoid being seen. I could see that Krissy wanted to confront them but I had to encourage her not to "No Krissy, I've told you before, we can't fight these people, these are farmers and fishermen they are not fighters."

The village mob passed us without seeing us so we then slowly moved down the path towards the docks. Although it had been a while since we were last here, I knew exactly where the boat was. We walked through the woods and safely made it to the docks. The boat was there, exactly where we had left it. It was a little bit worse for wear as it hadn't been touched in over a year but it still looked in good enough condition to sail.

We put all our belongings into the boat and then I heard Krissy speak "This is the boat, the boat to take us east? surely there's another?" "No there isn't, she's a good boat, she'll get us to where we need to go." they had just finished loading the boat when they could hear shouting coming from up in the village. They then saw a line of torches heading their way. It looked like a snake of fire moving through the dark. "There they are, quickly before they get away."

They quickly unhitched the boat and pushed it out to sea away from the shallow waters. With the winds currently not blowing strong enough they each grabbed an oar and started to row as fast as they could. The boat was soon in deeper water and with each pull of the oars they found themselves safely moving away from the mob that was now stood on the waters edge.

Return Of The Bloodstone

Chapter 5

Using the oars we pulled the boat through the water as hard and as fast as we could. I couldn't remember rowing being such a difficult task. The coastal shore was slowly but surely appearing to get smaller and smaller. We continued to row the boat through the unusually steady seas. As soon as we were far enough out to sea we noticed that the winds had slightly picked up. It was at this point that we were able to raise the sails and as the wind caught them we changed our heading and started to sail east.

I knew this part of the northern seas well but I had never sailed past the northern point of land. Father always told us that should anything sail past the northern point then it would never return. He would tell us that anything that went past that point would be lost to the seas or worse it would be taken by what lives in them.

The winds had eventually started to pick up even more strength and we soon found ourselves sailing fast and freely eastward in search of the unknown. We had just past the northern point of land and I had to try my hardest not to show any fear. Krissy and Sloan were sat still in the boat just talking about what they think may lay ahead of us while myself and Athian were doing our best to ensure we kept the boat sailing eastward.

We managed to keep the boat on the same heading and we were moving at a decent pace. We must have been sailing for several hours, the strangest thing was that we saw nothing, no sea birds, no land, no other boats just open waters and the fresh sea air. I noticed that there were still some fishing nets and lines in the boat from the last time we used them. I decided to drop the lines to see if we could catch any fish. I had forgotten the taste of fresh fish, the opportunity to taste it again was too good of one to pass by. Unfortunately I couldn't bait the hooks with any regular bait as it had completely shrivelled and dried out. I decided to use some of the meat from our rations. I should of thought to check the house for any bait when we were there but with what had happened I didn't have time to even think about it yet alone to gather fish bait.

The lines were being dragged for at least an hour and we didn't manage to catch anything but I didn't let that stop me from trying. I kept pulling the lines in and dropping them out again, all in the hope of catching something. I had done this several times and I hadn't caught one fish, it must have been the bait. Usually I'm able to catch something by dropping baited lines, but on this occasion it wasn't working.

I let the others sleep while I was doing this, I was trying my best to keep the boat on the correct heading. Luckily it was dark so using the stars made it much easier to navigate. The night sky had soon started to fade away from blackness. It was turning a dark blue before eventually getting lighter and lighter. In the horizon I could see the bright burning light of the sun as it was rising above the water. It's one of the most amazing things to witness, especially when out at sea either fishing or just sailing, seeing the morning sun rise above everything with nothing to obscure its power shows the world so clearly.

With such a sight I decided to wake the others so they could also gaze upon it's beauty. I was fairly certain that Krissy and Sloan may of never seen such a sunrise. I may have been wrong, but I was quite sure that this would be something new for them. "Sloan, Krissy, wake up, look at what a new day is bringing us." They both opened their eyes slowly and saw what I was pointing at. "Beautiful, absolutely Beautiful" said Krissy. Sloan just sat there staring at it and Athian raised his head slightly before sitting upright. He opened his eyes to see what it was. Once realising that it was just the sunrise he slumped his head back down on to the deck of the boat and decided to rest a little longer.

Several hours of the morning had passed and we managed to fully refresh ourselves and just as we were thinking that we had complete control of everything the skies had started to fill with clouds. Not the white clouds that you would usually see above a valley field but these were large dark grey and black clouds. I instantly knew what this meant and so did Athian. A storm was coming and a storm at sea brings multiple dangers. The waters started to get choppy and heavy and they made the boat rock from side to side. The waves were getting larger and larger and as such each one smashed against the boat with more force. As each wave hit the boat hard we all got caught in the onrushing water. No matter where we stood in the boat, the inrushing water and the constant rocking was forcing us to slip and fall.

We were starting to lose control of the boat, but with what nature was bringing us we did our best to cope. Then the worst thing that could of happened did. The winds had gained so much force that we struggled to stand at all. There was no way that I could control the boats boom in these winds. The mast was being blown so hard that the boat nearly capsized several times. The winds were now at near full strength and we all knew that the biggest danger in a sea storm were the winds that they bring. The winds were that strong we were starting to panic, we were struggling to do anything. Sloan even tried to help fight the storm by using magic but the wind force was too powerful and the waves had so much strength in them he was helpless to do a thing. Krissy suddenly spoke out "Don't fight nature, remember the elder told us, not to fight nature."

We all suddenly remembered what the elder had told us so we decided to grab what rope we could find and managed to secure ourselves to the boats deck. All we could do now was pray, pray for the storm to end. The boat was being thrown from left to right and us along with it. As the waves kept smashing the boat hard we could see parts of it starting to break away. I started to think back on all the times that I had been out to sea before and I couldn't remember a storm having as much force as this one. The winds had turned the boat around completely and they were forcing us away from the direction that were heading. We needed to go east but they appeared to be pushing us in a south westerly direction. There was nothing we could do to stop it.

There appeared to be no end to this storm. It was throwing everything it could at us, trying it's best to destroy the very thing we needed to survive. I then realised that to ease the pressure being forced upon the boat I had to drop the sails. I should of lowered the sails as soon as I noticed the storm starting but it had completely slipped my mind.

All that was in my mind now was that I had to drop the sails. It was the only thing that I could think of doing to relieve the danger that we currently in. I untied myself from the secure latching and tried my hardest to move towards the mast. The sheer force and strength of the storm kept pushing me back with every step that I took. As I was finally making some headway towards the mast I heard a loud snapping sound and as I looked up to see what it was the mast came smashing down on to the deck narrowly missing me. It had completely snapped into two with the top half swinging wildly across the boat. The swinging half of the mast was causing more damage to the boat than what the storm was. I managed to fight my way through the wind and the waves and I was able to grab hold of a sail rope. Holding the rope as tightly as I could with one hand I took out my knife with the other. Holding the rope tightly I started to cut through it the best I could. The rope was quite weak and my blade sliced through it quite easily. Once the rope was severed I was hoping to see the mast released but it wasn't, it was still attached and it was still swinging about causing damage to the boat.

I eventually grabbed the second rope and tried to release it. This rope appeared to be much tougher than the first and I was struggling to cut through it. I had to apply more force and as I did this the knife slipped down my hand slicing deep into my palm. With the pain this caused I lost grip of the knife and it dropped to the deck. A wave then came crashing into the boat and washed the knife to the opposite side, luckily it didn't wash it overboard.

The ropes that were keeping the snapped mast attached had to be cut. I decided that I had to try and retrieve the knife. The other's stayed securely attached to the boat and just watched on as I did my best to ensure us a little more safety. I had an idea that the best way to get to the knife was to let the water wash me to where it was. As a wave hit the boat I released my grip and found myself being forced to the opposite side of the boat. The water forced me across the deck so fast and hard that I was very nearly washed overboard. After recovering myself I started to look around the deck of the boat and that's when I saw the knife. It was wedged into a crack on the boats side, I leaned my arm out as far as I could in an attempt to reach it, but it was too far from my reach. I started to stretch my body out as far as I could but I still wasn't able to reach it. Just as I was about to pull my arm back in the boat swung to the other side and the knife was released from where it was wedged, it was being washed my way and was heading towards me. I quickly moved my hand down in the direction of its path and was able to grab the knife as it was about to pass me. I held on to it as tightly as I could. Blood was dripping heavily from my hand so I had to hold the knife with my weaker one but I didn't let this stop me from doing what needed to be done.

I managed to fight my way back to the other side of the boat and once I had steadied myself I was able to I grab the last rope that needed to be cut free. I wasn't as efficient with the knife in my weaker hand but I started to cut through the rope as quickly as I could. As the knife eventually passed through the rope I saw that the mast was free. I had done it, the ropes were finally cut and as one big wave smashed onto the boat the mast slid off and into the sea. I quickly made my way back towards where the others were and managed to secure myself once more.

The storm appeared to be never ending, nature was

constantly unleashing its brutal force upon us. Krissy was screaming in fear but with the noise of the wind and the waves smashing against the boat we could barely hear her. Sloan was still trying to use his magic to reduce the battering force but it was no good. He couldn't keep any concentration long enough to cast any spells. All we could do was hold on as tightly as we could and for as long as we could.

The storm must have been delivering it's punishment upon us for several hours, I'm sure that I could hear a slight crying, it was either Krissy or Athian but there was nothing more that I could do for them. We all felt tired and completely exhausted, we then noticed that the storm had started to ease. The waves eventually reduced to small splashes against the boat before stopping completely. The winds had stopped blowing and the clouds above us in the sky started to disperse before completely disappearing and again revealing a clear blue sky with the sun shining bright.

The storm had finally finished, it was over. We had all survived the horror that nature had unleashed upon us. None of us came out of the storm unscathed, we were all carrying cuts and bruises, luckily nothing too serious, apart from the slice in my palm. I managed to clean the wound up the best that I could before then wrapping it. I had to tear part of my shirt to use for the wrapping but I didn't care, the important thing was that we were all together and we were all alive.

Return Of The Bloodstone

The sea had completely settled and it was now so calm that it barely had a ripple in it. There were no waves hitting the boat at all, it was strange for there to be no waves but after this encounter we didn't stop to question as to why. But this now brought us a new problem, with no water movement the boat was completely static, it wasn't drifting at all, there was no rocking, nothing at all, we were completely motionless.

We had to get the boat moving, we tried using our hands to get some forward momentum going but the boat still appeared to be staying still. We looked around the boat for the oars but we couldn't find them. They were no where to be seen, we must of lost them while the boat was being battered by the storm. With the mast snapping and having to be cut away we had no sails. We were stranded, stranded in the middle of nowhere and unable to move.

"What now?" asked Krissy "I don't know, I honestly don't know." All of us looked at each other before Sloan spoke "now we go down. We must remember what the elder had told us to do. We must go to where nature takes us and when we can go no further we were to go down." He was right, nature had brought us to this point and we could go no further. The only thing beneath us was the deep blue sea. I didn't know these parts of the waters and I didn't know all the dangers out here but I did know one danger that exists in all seas, sharks. I wasn't sure where we were or even if we were where we needed to be. Did we need to be elsewhere? Were we in the right place? These questions kept going around in my head and I didn't know the answers.

We all sat still in the boat for a while, not too sure of what we should do next. Sloan tried to use a movement force spell but it didn't work. All the magical effects happened as they were meant to but the boat still didn't move. Looking out into the distance around us we saw something that appeared to be land, there was a group of islands. They all looked circular in shape and each one had what appeared to be a mountainous peak in it's centre.

Athian had been really quiet since the storm stopped but he then decided to speak "If we could reach those islands then maybe we could have a chance." The only problem with what Athian had said was that they were too far away. They were definitely too far for us to safely swim to and with no sails or wind the boat was static, we only had the one choice, we had to go down, down into the sea and hopefully find what we were searching for.

I started to look at the others and I could see fear in all of their eyes. I had to say something to bring back some high spirits "So down it is then" Athian looked at me in shock "Really? Down? How are we meant to go down?" "I don't know Athian but we need to think of a way." Let's see how far down we can swim."

I decided to take off off my jacket and asked Krissy to hold it for me. I stood to my feet and jumped straight in to the water. I took one big deep breath and submersed myself underwater. I then started to make my descent downwards. It was hard to clearly see at first but once my eyes had adjusted to the difference in light it was actually quite clear. I could see several large fish swimming around individually while all the smaller fish were swimming in shoals. They were moving together in fast darting patterns, keeping themselves away from anything that threatened them. I tried my hardest to see how far down I could swim before having to surface for air. I noticed that as I got deeper down in to the depths of the sea it got darker and darker making it more difficult to see what was in its murky depths.

It had been a while since I was last swimming at such a depth. I can clearly remember the last time, how could I ever forget such a time, after all it's what led to me losing my father.

I had to keep returning to the waters surface multiple times, allowing myself to take in good deep breaths of air. Each time I surfaced I told the others exactly what I could see below. Every time I searched I was able to swim that little bit deeper than the previous attempt. I had to ask Sloan exactly what it was that I was looking for. He told me that I had to search for a large chest and that it would have cast iron chains wrapped around it. The chest would have ancient writing carved in to it's sides.

So each time searching I tried my best to look in different areas. This was all I could think of doing in order not to miss anywhere. The last thing I wanted to do was to keep searching in the same place. I kept looking for as long as I could but I couldn't find anything, It was pointless. After many failed attempts I surfaced and climbed back in to the boat. After shaking the water off of myself I started to doubt that we were even in the right place. Sloan was looking directly at me before speaking "I will try to look, it's been down there for a thousand years so it wont be easy to see." I was a bit concerned if Sloan could hold his breath as long as what I could so I had to give him warning "Sloan, you have to go quite deep, are you able to hold your breath long enough?" "Don't worry Mickel, I won't need to." Sloan took off his outer clothing leaving his weapons strapped to himself and jumped in to the sea. He was just floating in the water, he didn't make any attempt to swim down in search for the chest, then suddenly he started to speak and an incantation while treading the water. A light then started to appear around his body. It was strange, the water was being forced away from his skin. He was in the water surrounded by this light, a light that was keeping him the water away from him, It was as if he was in a giant air bubble. He then suddenly submerged himself under the water and was moving downwards towards the dark depths. From up in the boat we could see the light down below. With this magical light around him he was able to breathe and move freely in the watery depths. "Wow, I wonder if I could do that." "Athian, I'm sure you're not to that level yet." I kept thinking how selfish of him, if he could do that then why did he leave me to search for so long.

Return Of The Bloodstone

Krissy was just leaning over the edge of the boat, trying to see if she could see Sloan, but he was now too deep and the light had completely faded from sight. I was drying myself off and Athian was trying to perform the same magic trick that Sloan had just done, only as with most of his magical attempts he failed yet again.

Sloan now surrounded by his magical orb was deep beneath the sea looking for anything that appeared to be an old sunken boat. He knew that if he had any chance of finding the chest then it was going to be amongst a wreckage. With him using his magic he didn't need to surface for air, this gave him plenty of time to look around for the chest, but he had to find the right area. Checking all the raised areas at the sea bed he found nothing that resembled a wreckage.

We were all thinking the same thing, and that was where could the chest be? They had listened to the elders and they survived the storm that nature thrust upon them. They were now at the point where they could go no further, It had to be down there somewhere, but where? Sloan was freely moving around at the bottom of the sea. He was disturbing the sand which had probably never been touched before. He had to find a way to aid his search. Then he remembered something that would help with him. He remembered a spell that would reveal magical Items.

Sloan with the magical force around him was stood on the bed of the sea, he closed his eyes and attempted the spell. In the ancient language he started to speak and as he opened his eyes he spoke to himself "Reveal yourself unto me." He had now opened his eyes fully and started to look around, he saw that everything in front of him was exactly as it was before. There was nothing magical in front of him. He started to look in all directions, checking everywhere, but he still couldn't see anything that appeared to be of magical origin. He decided to move further away from the boat and look in different places. As he moved further away, he appeared to be heading towards what looked like underwater caves. He got closer and closer to the caves and he then noticed that there was a light coming from inside of them. A slight glimmering light reflecting in the water from the cave's entrance could be seen. Could this be it? Could he of found what he was looking for.

We stayed in the boat waiting for Sloan to reappear but as of yet he hadn't returned. We tried to look through the water to see if we could see him but we couldn't, he was completely out of sight. Krissy then spoke to us "I think we may need to go and look for him." "Krissy, I'm a good swimmer but I won't be able to hold my breath long enough." We decided to stay in the boat and wait a little longer. While we were waiting we managed to repair some of the damage caused by the storm, however even though the boat was in better repair we were still unable to move.

Meanwhile in the depths of the sea Sloan had made his way to the entrance of the cave. He could now see the light more clearly and as he got closer to it the colour changed from a light yellow to a red glow. Slowly making his way into the cave he moved closer and closer towards the light. As he got further into the cave the water had started to disappear from beneath him, he was soon walking on rock with no water around him at all, the cave was full of air. He soon found himself in a large open area of the cave and as he was able to breathe freely so he removed the shielding spell from around himself.

He could see that in the middle of the opening he found there was a bright beaming red light. He moved closer towards it to enable himself to clearly see what it was. He was now stood right in-front of the light, he had found it, he had found the Bloodstone. He bent down to pick up the chest, wrapping one hand around the back of it and pulling it close to his body. As he turned to leave the cave he heard something moving. Something was moving in the shadows of the cave, he wasn't alone. Whatever was in there with him was hiding, it was hiding from sight and slowly moving around in the darkness. In an attempt to leave he decided to make his way back toward the cave entrance.

While attempting to leave he was slowly looking around the cave but he wasn't able to see anything. He then started to make his way closer towards the cave entrance and that's when he heard it again. There was definitely something in there with him. The sounds it made were that of something moving around in the darkness, dragging itself across the rough stone floor of the cave.

Return Of The Bloodstone

Sloan knew that he had to leave and that he had to leave now. As he was walking towards the entrance he felt a breeze fall upon him. He again looked around the cave as something didn't feel right. While he was holding the chest he noticed that the illuminating light that had been shining from within had started to fade, It was at this moment he felt a presence, he didn't feel alone, he knew now that something was in there with him and it didn't want him to leave.

He again heard the sound of something being dragged across stone and it was slowly moving out of the darkness, making it's way towards him. Moving out of the darkness he could see what appeared to be two golden lights. They moved closer towards him, slowly moving out of the shadows and into the light, he then realised what they were, they were eyes, they were the eyes of whatever it was that had been watching him from the darkness. Sloan didn't want to stay in cave long enough to find out what they belonged to so he was rushing to make his way out. He was nearly there when the beast that was in there with him raced past him and blocked his exit. Sloan wasn't able to move quickly enough and he soon found himself stood face to face with the beast that was hidden in the dark, It was a dragon. A water dragon, the protector of the Bloodstone.

Chapter 6

The Swamplands had now started to fall under the shroud of Blaine's black cloud. Nearly half of them were in darkness and allowing the demons to move forth and to kill or force out it's inhabitants. Davos and Delia had lost many city guards and loyal common folk while attempting to take control of the swamp. Deep into the swamp corpses from both the swamp creatures that lived there and Blaine's legion could be seen scattered everywhere.

All different types of beasts were slain by the demons that moved forth, the demons could be seen in the darkness feasting on the bodies that were left to rot. A terrible stench of decay hung in the air adding a spooky eeriness that was already part of these lands.

As the cloud was now over most of the swamp it wouldn't be long before it was soon completely enshrouded in darkness. With Davos knowing that the wastelands were not far away, he decided to return to the city with Delia.

He ordered the legion to travel no further until the swamps were in complete darkness. The guards set up camps at the edge of the swamp while the unholy beasts and demons hid themselves in the darkness, all that could be seen of them were their piercing red eyes as they lay in wait.

Davos and Delia both knew that Blaine wouldn't want to hear excuses but they also knew that if he wasn't kept informed then he would unleash his fury upon them. It didn't take them long for them to return to the city. As the both of them are now much stronger they tend to use their magical abilities more often. This is allowing them to have a superior advantage over man, they could disappear and reappear as they pleased aiding them in their much needed travels.

They quickly arrived at the temple and started to make their way towards the temple hall. Once they arrived in the hall they could see that Blaine sat in his throne. They slowly approached him to inform him of their efforts. As they got closer to their master they were suddenly confronted by one of his guardians. A demon hound was stood directly in front of them growling with it's viscous intent towards them. With its deep growl constantly rumbling it was staring directly at them with a lust for blood in it's eyes. With one wave of Blaine's hand it simply stopped growling, turned and walked away. They were both then able to continue further towards Blaine. As they got close enough to their master they lowered their heads and knelt before him.

Return Of The Bloodstone

"Where is the Legion? What lands are yet to be taken?" "We are part way through the swamp master, the legion are waiting on the edge of the swamp lands for our return. We must wait for the swamp to be in complete darkness before we can take full control." Blaine rose to his feet banging his staff down hard, and as he did this an almighty clash of thunder could be heard from overhead. "We are not moving fast enough, this world should be mine by now. People or living creatures of this world should not be a reason for delay. Go, get me full control of the swamp and do not return until this is done." Blaine then suddenly disappeared from site leaving the demon hounds and a black mist in the air behind him.

Davos and Delia both left the temple as quickly as they could knowing that his guardians were there without their master to control them. They made their way out of the temple and into the city centre. There they could see the black smoke filling the air from the arena. Delia decided to stay in the city and advised Davos to return to the legion and prepare them for a long march through the swamp."Night will soon be amongst us, move the legion forth through the swamp and towards the wastelands." "What do you intend on doing Delia?" "I intend on spreading the lords darkness faster, now go."

Davos then faded into a mist and vanished from the city. Delia made her way to the Arena and placed herself at it's highest point. She was looking down into the arena staring right into the Vortex. The demons and creatures that had been coming from within had all but nearly stopped arriving. What Delia intended on doing was to increase the smoke that was constantly being drawn into our world. She started to speak an incantation after a few moments a wind starting to stir inside the arena. As the wind picked up in pace and power it started to pull more smoke from the vortex and was soon a strong swirling whirlwind, similar to those that the night brings in the wastelands.

The smoky fog was starting to get thicker and thicker, it was a near total black in colour, Delia started to push the cloud out of the arena and into the already darkened skies above her. She started to force the dark clouds northward but at a faster pace. Her plan was working, she was pushing the dark shroud north and areas that were still in the natural night sky soon had the appearance of an unholy darkness.

While Delia was carrying out her own method of intervention Davos was back with the legion on the swampland borders. He noticed that the intensity of the dark clouds were getting thicker and that they were moving faster. As he was witnessing this change he prepared the unholy legion and started to march them through the swamps. Any inhabitants of the swamp that they encountered were soon met by the advancing city guards and the demonic beasts that moved with them.

It didn't take them long to move through where they had already been and in a short while they soon found themselves moving through the northern part of the swamp coming across very little resistance. With the cloud now being forced northwards at a faster pace Delia left the arena and rejoined Davos in the swamps. When she arrived she saw several large reptilian beasts defending themselves against the city guards. She had to protect the guards as they were needed to be the front line soldiers for any daylight advances. Using her magical abilities she called forth What appeared to be lightning bolts from her hands, striking down the swamp creatures with ease as they attempted to attack the guards. As the giant reptiles lay wounded on the ground the demons were quick to take advantage and started to sink their sharp teeth and claws deep into their scaly hides. biting, pulling and ripping chunks of flesh from them.

The legion was strong, with dark magic, demons and man combined they had managed to fight their way through the swamps with ease. They found themselves standing on the edge of the wastelands, not daring to enter them until ordered to do so. Everything behind them was now dead or dying. Oil pits from the swamp could be seen burning larger and brighter than before as bodies were thrown into them forced the flames to spread onto any trees that were still stood standing. This was something that hasn't happened for a millennium, the oil pits usually burn with a low flame, providing heat and a little light for what lives in the swamplands, never changing, always burning at a constant level.

With all the fighting and killing they didn't realise that the night hours were nearly all consumed. They had marched past the safe haven of night and as the sun started to rise in the sky and its light brightening up the lands screams of pain and agony could be heard from the demons that had advanced too far. Davos and Delia tried their best to get as many of them back but they had a hunger to kill within them, they wanted to bring more chaos and destruction as quickly as they could and to whatever they could.

They soon had to learn for themselves of the dangers that lay ahead of them. As they kept rushing forwards many of them combusted into flames and ash as they ran into the natural light of the sun. The shadow demons were the first to realise that they could go no further and others soon followed their lead and contained their blood-lust.

They were now on the border of the wastelands, with darkness behind them and light in front of them, the demons needed to wait one more day before they could advance any further.

What Davos didn't know was that with Delia intervening with the spread of the dark cloud she had created a void of darkness in the skies, she had forced it to move too quickly, thinning the cloud out in many parts. The burnt out villages and forests that once stood outside of the city were once again exposed to sunlight. With natural light again touching these lands it started to return life into them, shoots of grass could be seen piercing through the ash covered ground and saplings from the burnt trees could be seen appearing from the ground around from. The green life that once covered this land had slowly started to return. Blaine had noticed that areas of the skies had somehow became open and allowed light to protrude through his dark cloud. All those around him could see the rage and fury upon in his face, he let out such a loud and furious scream that it could be heard throughout the city. The constant rumbling of thunder above the city had now ceased. The ever flowing vacuum of black smoke coming from the vortex had now became thinner and the blackness in the skies above the city had started to fade. The change of the world being imposed by Blaine had been interrupted. With so much fury now within him he left the city and ported himself and his demon guardians to the borders of the swamp and the wastelands. He soon sought out the whereabouts of Davos and Delia and saw that they were planning their next advance. They both noticed Blaine in their presence and fear could be seen to instantly come across their faces. Blaine stood staring at them both with anger and hatred upon his face "What have you done?" They both weren't too sure why their master was so furious but they knew that something had happened, something that neither of them were not prepared for. The look on Delia's facial expression had changed, she knew, she knew why Blaine had left the temple and sought them out, she knew the reason as to why he was amongst them.

As he got closer to them he asked them one question "Which one of you intervened? Which one of you took it upon yourself to interfere with the vortex?" They were both kneeling before their master, neither of them were saying a word. Without even speaking Blaine had them both holding their heads and screaming in pain. Once Blaine had finished inflicting his punishment upon them he again spoke "Now which one of you intervened?" Once the inflicted pain had ceased Delia decided to speak. "I only gave it push master, you wanted the swamps under full control, so to give you the world faster I cast an elemental spell upon the vortex. I wanted to thicken the cloud and push it north at a faster rate." Blaine raised his hand and pointed his finger at Delia. As he did this one of the demon hounds approached her, it was growling heavily and had drool dripping from its mouth, all of its razor sharp teeth were on show. She was knelt in front of her master not knowing what was going to happen next. She was thinking that she had to get away, she tried to use an incantation to escape but she wasn't able to cast one. She then thought that maybe an apology and an explanation might help her, as she went to speak a demon hound pounced on her biting at tearing the flesh from the back of her neck. As Delia's body lay on the ground be ripped apart Davos quickly moved himself away to what he was hoping to be a safer distance. The second hound then started to approach, all types of thoughts were going through Davos's mind, he was thinking that he was the next to be brutally killed. The second hound then launched itself forward towards Davos, it snapped its jaws together loudly before turning away from him and starting to rip flesh from the remains of Delia's body as it lay motionless on the bloodied ground. As the hounds were feasting upon the body Blaine lowered his hand and both of the demons ceased their feeding.

Blaine stood over what remained of Delia and was staring down at her. Davos had now realised the true fury of his dark master, he took this as a lesson learnt not to disappoint him. With blood flowing heavily from the ripped apart corpse it seeped into ground turning the soil to a near black shade. Blaine stood staring at her for a while longer, he then turned away from her body and took several steps away before speaking "Mercy is for the weak." The demon hounds again pounced on Delia's body and started to rip it into pieces. They each grabbed a limb and pulled them from her corpse with ease. Davos stood watching from a distance not daring to intervene or to even speak. Blaine continued to walk away and before disappearing into complete darkness Davos heard him speak "Pull the legion back into the swamp, no more advancing of the legion until I can fix this." Blaine then disappeared from site taking his demon guards with him.

Davos gathered the legion and started to move them back into the swamplands away from the dangers of the sunlight that was currently shining into the wastelands. Bodies were lay strewn and scattered across all the lands that they had walked through. The demons had certainly brought with them death, destruction and chaos. Davos decided to bring the legion back to the south side of the swamp. As they moved further south they could all notice that the dark clouds above the southern skies were now lighter than they were previously and rays of sunlight could seen shining through multiple sections of the clouds. He now understood why Blaine was so furious and had carried out the actions that he did. His main concern now was that with Delia gone he was on his own, and as such he felt personally weaker, he needed more support, he needed another warlock or witch that would be willing to help him, willing to support him should he ever need it, one that was willing to protect him.

Blaine had returned to the vortex and was trying to repair the damage that Delia had caused. He started to speak the incantation that he used to open the vortex but there was no difference. He then tried an alternate spell to draw out the darkness that was deep below, but again this led to failure. No matter how hard he tried he couldn't return the flow of blackness from the vortex. He needed more power, knowing his powers alone were not strong enough he had to have the help of others. Davos had more powers than he knew, he needed Davos with him in the arena. He was hoping that with their combined powers that they would again be able to drain the darkness from one realm into his.

He looked up to the skies and could see the blackness above the city had already started to fade. Although no sunlight was currently shining through into the city he knew that it was only a matter of time. There was already one area of land that was exposed to sunlight and this exposed area had started to become larger moving further north behind the dark cloud. If this moved too far then the unholy legion would be at risk, they would be at risk of death from the sunlight that would soon be upon them.

With Blaine not being able to draw any more darkness from the vortex he opened a portal to where Davos was and summoned him to come through it to him. It didn't take Davos long and he was soon in the arena before his master. "Yes master, how can I be of service?" "We need to repair the damage caused by your sister. Now speak as I do and focus on the vortex. Focus all your inner deep dark energy into the centre of the vortex and call it to come forth."

They were both speaking in an ancient language, chanting and calling forth what lay deep within the vortex. After a short while the life in the fires that were coming from the vortex once again started to flicker. The flames had started to grow higher and the dark red light that illuminated from the vortex could again be seen. Blaine knew that he still needed more power to successfully draw out the darkness from the other realm. During the last calling there were three of them, but now with just the two they weren't strong enough. Blaine needed the dark smoke from the other realm to bleed it's way into his world, although the fires were burning and growling of demonic beasts could be heard coming from the vortex, there was still no black smoke being drawn into the world. They weren't able to call forth what they wanted. Blaine decided to stop the incantation and told Davos to return to the legion. "Go, protect the legion. light is breaking through and we can't lose our hold on the lands that we have claimed."

The skies above the arena had now started to clear of the dark black shroud that was once filling them. Sunlight had eventually managed to break through and was once again shining on to parts of the city. As it shone brightly into the city it clearly showed the horrors that had happened there. All the different horrors and atrocities that took place under darkness were visual for all to see. Hundreds of bodies lay scattered across the ground, remains and body parts from what the demons didn't devour lay everywhere. The very soil and stone ground was puddled with the blood from the slaughtered innocent.

As sunlight was shining through into parts of the city the thick black roots that were exposed to it could be seen to start to wilt away. Blaine could do nothing, he needed more power at the vortex and he needed it now. His world had started to lose its shape. He needed more dark energy. In the temple he had several other dark masters to call upon but they were no where near powerful enough. He needed a gemstone. He needed a night stone or the ruby known as the eye of the dragon. He knew that the night stone would give him the ability to call forth demons and unholy monstrosities with ease. The night stone is full of darkness, full of evil and has so much power. He knew that the search for one would take too long, one had to be created. Created by magic to hold nothing but darkness and hate. The eye of the dragon ruby stone was one of the rarest ancient gemstones. It gave it's holder the power to change shape of things around him, it would allow anyone or anything to instantly be weakened or killed.

Blaine disappeared from the arena and found himself back in the temple hall. He called forth all his faithful warlocks and witches and ordered them to search the world for the lost scribes. Scribes which would tell him where to find the night stone or how one could be created. One by one the dark masters opened portals and disappeared through them vanishing from the temple. There was nothing else that he could do, time was against him. With the dark cloud in the skies now obtaining an open void his unholy legion was trapped. They could only move at night or move along with the cloud that was above them during the day. Either way his army was now limited to where they could go. They were limited to where they could cause chaos, death and destruction.

Chapter 7

We had been sat in the boat waiting for Sloan to surface with the ancient chest and the Bloodstone enclosed but it didn't happen. We didn't know what could have been keeping him or what was taking him so long. All we knew was that he had used magic to help him breathe underwater, but for how long his magic would last for and how long it would take, none of us knew. "What could be keeping him?" "I don't know Krissy, but I'm certain he will be fine." Athian was looking very worried, we both knew that he wanted to help but his acquired magical abilities were very limited. I decided that we should go and look for him.

I readied myself for another swim into the deep and asked the others if they wanted to come and help me search. I didn't get the response I was hoping for so I swam down on my own, swimming as far down as I could go hoping to see what was happening.

While diving as deep as I could go, I looked all around for any sight of Sloan. He wasn't to be seen anywhere in the depths directly beneath the boat or any of the surrounding area. I swam back to the surface and told the others that Sloan wasn't there, "I can't see him, come on, please help me. I can only look in one area at a time." I got a discontented look from the both of them, but then suddenly they both stood to their feet and removed the heavy items that they were wearing but kept their weapons on them. Krissy kept the daggers in the sheaf's, they were strapped around her legs and waist, she closed her eyes and jumped into the water. Athian removed most of his clothing and then soon joined us.

"Okay, where do you want us to search?" asked Athian. I decided that diving downwards wasn't the best method to search. We had to search further out, we each swam out away from the boat and once we were far enough from the boat we all acknowledged to each other that we were ready. Before I knew it Krissy had already submerged herself underwater and started to swim as deep down as she could go. Athian and I soon did the same thing, making sure that we all had sight of each-other.

We were all now searching the basin of the sea, each of us in different areas. It was dark and murky in the deep waters but we could still see each other, but only just. Each one of us was hoping to catch any sight of Sloan. If any of us were to see him then we were to confirm it when we surfaced for air.

As each of us were only able to hold our breath for a short while we had to keep surfacing multiple times.

When any one of us surfaced we made sure that we waited for the others to surface also. This way we were all looking out for each other.

We had made plenty of attempts in looking for Sloan but we couldn't see any sight of him anywhere. I was starting to think that this was pointless, that something had gone wrong. I thought I would ask Athian how much magic he actually knew. "Athian, what has Sloan taught you? Do you know enough magic to assist us?" He just looked over at me and didn't answer, he was too far away from me to clearly hear what I was asking him.

We all swam towards each-other and once we were close enough together I asked him the same question. "Athian, what has Sloan taught you, do you know a magical spell that can help us?" "He hasn't taught me everything, mostly just the basics." "Just the basics, what do you mean just the basics?" "You know like making light, moving objects, fire manipulation and tracking, those sort of things." I paused a short a while and thought about what Athian had just told us. "Tracking, you can track Sloan?" "Not too sure, it was a spell he taught me to track animals but I can give it a try." Athian was trying his hardest to stay afloat. He closed his eyes and was concentrating hard on the spell. He started to move his hands around in a circular motion but nothing was happening. He attempted it again for a second time but yet still nothing was happening.

Krissy then spoke "Do you not need to say anything?"

He opened his eyes and gave her a funny look "Do you want to try it? It's not as easy at it looks." we just stayed quiet from this point onwards and let him try again. After the third and fourth failed attempts he splashed the surface of the water with frustration. "I can't do it, I just can't do it." We had to encourage him not to give up. Without Sloan we would certainly be left out here to die.

The main problem that Athian had with magic was that he didn't gain all the knowledge as Sloan did. His Injuries weren't as severe as Sloan's and therefore only a little magic had entered his mind and blood. The rest of the learning and development had to come from him. Over time I'm sure he will develop it and become stronger, but we didn't have time, we needed him to focus now.

With a big sigh Athian once again closed his eyes and started to move his hands. This time we could see him concentrating harder than before. Then he actually started to speak "From in the darkness and out of sight, let me see my master's light." While concentrating hard with his eyes closed and moving his hands he repeated the same incantation over and over again, keeping his eyes closed the whole time and that's when it happened. A blue light started to form between his hands, he didn't open his eyes to see. He just kept speaking and concentrating. The light then got really bright and as Athian opened his eyes the light disappeared from his hands and into the water.

He looked over at Krissy and myself "Did it work? Did

anything happen?" Something happened Athian but we're not quite sure what." Mickel then submersed himself underwater and he could see that parts of the water below him were glistening, they were glistening with a light. After seeing this he resurfaced and told the others what he saw.

Due to them only being able to hold their breath for a short while they followed the trail the best they could from the waters surface. After continuously following the trail of light they realised that they were quite far from the boat. The trail of light that was deep in the water soon disappeared, they could no longer follow it from the surface. They all decided that this was the point in which they had to swim deep to continue tracking what they were following. They all took and a deep breath and submersed themselves under the surface. They swam downwards as quickly as they could to give themselves as much time as possible. Once they got near the sea bed they realised that the glistening light trail could once again be seen, they could see it clearly and it led into a cave. They were all managing to hold their breath well and decided to follow the light into the cave. As they entered the cave they soon realised that there was an air pocket above them. They each surfaced to take another deep breath before continuing their search for Sloan. As they swam through the water the space was getting narrow and before they knew it the water had become shallow and they soon found themselves in an air filled cavern.

As they stood in the open part of the cavern they heard a roar coming from within. This made them all stop and stare into the darkness wondering that was ahead of them. "What the heck was that?" shouted Athian. "I'm not too sure, but I think we need to go and find out." The look on Krissy's face wasn't one of fear or one of shock but more like a look of recognition, she knew what it was, she had heard a similar sound before. She didn't say a word to the other's on what she thought it might be, she just stood still quietly.

Now was the chance for Athian to again show us what he was capable of. He whispered a few words and suddenly a light orb appeared in front of him. He had managed to use his abilities and bring light into this blackness that we had currently found ourselves in. So that we didn't get lost in the darkness we stayed as close to him as we could.

We didn't have to walk far before we once again heard the loud roar, only this time it was accompanied by a voice, a human voice. The voice was shouting at whatever it was that was making the horrendous roars and growls. Ahead in the darkness of the cave noises that could be heard, there were also sounds of fighting, there was a battle taking place. I think we all knew who it was, but what he was battling with we didn't know. We got closer and closer until we were soon able to see a light ahead of us. The light was coming from what appeared to be a large opening in the cave.

Return Of The Bloodstone

As there was enough light coming from ahead of us Athian ceased his magical spell as it was no longer required. When he stopped the spell he appeared to be drained of energy, he was feeling tired and fatigued so he sat himself against the cold wet wall of the cave. To avoid being seen we made sure that we kept ourselves hidden in the shadows. We couldn't believe what we were witnessing, Sloan was in battle with a dragon. It wasn't as large as I thought a dragon would be, but either way it was a dragon. It was gold and green in colour and it had large claws at the end of each toe with each one being nearly the same size as my hand. It didn't have large wings like I thought dragons would have but instead they were much smaller, they looked more like fins, the sort of fins that you would expect to find on a shark. It's teeth were pure white and the sound of it's roar sent shivers through my whole body. It had multiple horns on its head and a line of smaller ones running down its spine. Athian was completely speechless, he was always amazed with the elders stories of mythical beasts, but to actually see one stood in-front of him had him nearly lost for words. "That's a, D D Dragon."I could see that he was scared but he wasn't moving, he was still feeling fatigued and was trying to gain back what strength he could.

We stayed hidden for a little while until Athian felt better and once he was able to we moved ourselves along the wall keeping hidden in the darkness. We stayed in the darkness watching the battle between Sloan and this beast, we still couldn't believe what we were seeing, a battle between Sloan and a dragon.

The dragon was stood in the centre of the cavern breathing it's dragon breath towards Sloan, it wasn't a red fire coming from its mouth but it was a blue fire. None of us had ever seen such a thing. Sloan was moving between the stalactites avoiding the flames that would surely burn him to cinders if struck by them. Every time Sloan managed to dodge the flames he also had to dodge the dragon's long scaly tail that was being whipped towards him.

He wasn't just avoiding the attacks, but he was also trying to attack himself. He was using his magic and casting his own spells against the dragon. He was trying many different incantations against the dragon but none of them appeared to have any effect on it. The fire that he was thrusting towards the dragon wasn't strong enough to cause it harm, it's overlapping scales were giving it full protection.

We were watching the battle so intently that I didn't even think that we should be out there assisting Sloan. "We have to help him" said Krissy, "But what can we do" I replied. Athian wasn't able to help, he was still recovering from using his magic. "I suppose we will have to help the best we can." I decided to move away from the other two and started to sneak as quietly as I could against the cave walls, keeping myself hidden from sight. I pulled my long dagger from it's sheaf and I was ready to defend myself, I was ready to help Sloan, ready to do whatever I could.

As I moved quietly towards Sloan I noticed that Krissy had also prepared herself for a fight, with a dagger in each hand she was moving to the other side of the cave. Like myself, she was also using the shadows to keep herself hidden from sight. With her wearing nearly all black it was difficult for me to even see her, It was only the little flashes of gold from her hair and the silver flashes from her daggers that allowed me to see where she was. I had positioned myself in a place that gave me good clear vision of Sloan and the dragon. Sloan was trying his best to defend himself but the dragon was being relentless, whipping it's tail around the cave smashing the stalactites causing rock and debris to scatter across the cave. The dragon was constantly breathing its fire in an attempt to turn Sloan to dust. I had to do something, but what could I do? I noticed that there was a ledge in my part of the cave. Quietly moving around in the shadows I managed to climb this ledge. All I needed now was for the dragon to move closer to me. I was hoping that If I could jump on to the dragon then I might be able to thrust my dagger deep into its neck, hopefully I could harm it enough to invoke fear from us and make it retreat.

I had to get Sloan's attention, I started to throw small rocks down towards him. The first rock that I threw didn't go far enough so I kept throwing them hoping that he would see me. After several more attempts Sloan had finally managed to notice me. He had to reposition himself in the battle and try to encourage the dragon to come to my side of the cave. Sloan was doing the best that he could to avoid the rocks, fire and brute physical force of the dragon. On the other-side of the cave Krissy was slowly moving in the darkness of the shadows, ensuring that she kept completely out of sight. It took a while but Sloan had done it, I'm not sure how, but he had managed to move from the opposite side of the cave across to mine and he had brought the fiery beast with him. The dragon was getting closer and closer to me as Sloan moved directly below me and the ledge the dragon followed. The dragon thrust itself forward towards us. Sloan quickly moved away from ledge that I was stood on and the dragon was now directly below me. As the dragon turned I saw that this was my opportunity. I was scared, very scared. I kept thinking to myself what was I doing, I can't do this. I saw the base of the dragons skull and the top of his neck, this is where I needed to thrust my dagger. I closed my eyes and with one meaningful jump I launched myself downwards from the ledge and onto the dragon. Holding my dagger as tightly as I could and keeping the tip pointing downwards as I made my descent. I landed directly where I needed to be, my dagger started to pierce it's way through the scaly covering of the dragons neck. A mighty roar came from the beast as the silver blade of my dagger sunk its way deep in it.

The dragon started to thrust it's body and tail from left to right, smashing everything that it came into contact with. There was a constant flow of fire coming from it's large gaping jaws and as it thrust its body upwards in an attempt to throw me from it's back the stalagmites above us were being smashed to pieces. As they fell from the top of the cave the others were at risk of being crushed by the debris that was raining down around them. With one big thrust upwards from the dragon I felt a sharp pain to the back of my head as I was smashed against the roof of the cave which had now started to crumble. The dragon had managed to fling me from it's back and I fell to the base of cave hard.

Athian had now managed to recover and saw what was happening. He rushed across to where I was laying and saw that I was holding my head in pain. He managed to pull me away to the side of the cave, moving me to safety away from the debris that was falling from above. Sloan had been caught by some of the falling debris and was slightly trapped, he trying was trying his best to move the rocks off of himself so that he could move freely. As we were all trying to recover ourselves we felt a breeze blowing down against us. I was hoping that it was a wind from somewhere but I knew exactly what it was, it was the dragon, it was breathing heavily and growling loudly as it approached us. It got to within striking distance of us and was stood staring down at us. It lifted it's neck high and tilted it's head down backwards and let out a mighty roar. It then started to swallow the air fast, we could see a glow from the fire forming in it's throat. This was it, we had come so close to obtaining what we had sought, for it to now fail and end in disaster.

The dragon was walking slowly in front of them moving from side to side with it's fiery breath ready to launch down upon them all. As it lifted it's head high with a deep breath within it we closed our eyes thinking that this was it, this was where our lives ended. As we had our eyes closed and expecting the worst we heard a mighty roar, but we didn't feel the heat of the flames, or the breeze from the dragons breath, we weren't sure why so we opened our eyes and what we saw had shocked us all. It was Krissy, she was now facing off against the dragon. For every whip from the dragon's tail she managed to counter it with a quick avoidance move and as she did this she managed to stab the dragon with her piercing blades. Every time the dragon attempted to draw breath to create it's fire she inflicted pain upon it by slicing deep with her razor sharp daggers, She was trying to always slice across it's throat or neck. For every attack the dragon attempted she managed to match it and countered with an attack of her own.

The dragon was unable to inflict any harm upon her, she was too quick and too brutal with her counter attacks, The dragon knew that it was being matched and as such it started to back away from her. With Krissy realising this she kept concentrating hard on the battle that she had found herself in. She was able to force the dragon backwards, back into the dark shadows of the cave from where it came. I was thinking how is this possible, how is it possible for her to fight such a beast, then I heard Sloan speak. "Her trials, she passed her trial's. It's the abilities she gained on defeating the black dragon," That's when I remembered her telling me her story, how she gained the physical skills of the dragon, she defeated a black dragon in her trials and as such had the ability to defend us and fight what we were now up against. The battle lasted for several more minutes, this gave us time to recover slightly from what the beast had inflicted upon us.

Eventually the dragon had been forced back into the dark depths of the cave. Once it was away and out of sight Krissy rushed back to where we were, making sure that we were all okay. She told us that we needed to hurry. Athian was just staring at her intently before speaking "Wow, absolutely amazing," Sloan had managed to free himself from the rubble that he was trapped under. He didn't waste any time in doing so either, he freed himself quite quickly, dusted himself down and helped us to our feet. He was bleeding heavily from his arm but he was still able to help us to our feet, "Quickly, we must find the Bloodstone before the beast returns"

With everything that was happening with the dragon we had completely forgotten about the Bloodstone and it was now somewhere in the rubble. "Athian, bring us some light to assist us in our search," Athian then started to chant an incantation which again brought forward a bright burning orb before him. This gave the rest of us clear vision to assist in the search.

We were searching everywhere, we were lifting rocks and moving as much of the debris as we could. We had been searching for a few moments before we could again feel a breeze falling upon us, It wasn't just the breeze but we could also hear it moving from the darkness of the cave. We started to speed up our search knowing that the dragon could return at any moment. We then heard a deep growl coming from the dark depths of the cave. It was returning, the dragon was moving back towards us, it was moving forth out of the darkness that Krissy had forced it into. Just as the dragons eyes were becoming visible from the dark Sloan called out "I've found it, come we must leave now, and we must leave fast." We all started to look for the exit from the cave, it was difficult to find as the cave looked nothing like it did when we entered it. The hanging Stalactites were still crumbling and debris was still falling around us, the Stalagmites formed from the base of the cave were now all smashed to pieces.

We continued to look for the way out of the cave, the whole time we could hear the dragon getting closer and closer. "It's here, it's over here," Athian had managed to find the passage and all of us moved across to where he was. Looking at what Athian had found we were relieved to see that he was right, he had found the way out. We quickly moved the rubble that was blocking our way and entered the exit. As we were moving through the exit we heard a mighty thud against the inside of the cave. The dragon was trying to force it's way into the passage behind us. Luckily for us it was too large to fit, but this didn't stop it from trying. It was ramming it's body hard against the cave wall. The passage had started to give way and collapse behind us. We continued to move along the passage as quickly as we could. We could again feel water beneath our feet, we knew then that we were nearly out of the cave.

As the water got deeper and deeper we started to swim as fast as we could. We all swam frantically from the cave and once we were clear from the entrance we pushed ourselves upwards and swam straight to the surface. Athian was the first one to the surface, then it was Sloan followed by myself. I looked around to see where Krissy was but I couldn't see her. I started to look below the water's surface to catch any glimpse of her but I still couldn't see where she was, she wasn't beneath us. "Sloan, Krissy, where's Krissy?" "Swim to the boat Mickel, I will search for her." We started to swim towards the boat while Sloan stayed behind looking for any sign of Krissy. The boat wasn't directly above us so we had to swim as quickly as we could to get to safety. Once there Athian and myself pulled ourselves safely into the boat.

We lay on the boat and managed to recover enough to slightly relax. Leaning over the side and looking out across the water's surface we could see Sloan swimming towards us. I couldn't see Krissy with him but then as he got closer and turned there she was, he had found her. She had one of her arms around his neck with the other one tightly grasping an old chest. Once they got to the

115

boat we pulled them both up and into safety.

With everything that had just happened in the depths of the sea we all sat looking at each-other in disbelief. "Now what I asked?" Sloan was quick to reply "Now we go to Paradise" As he said this I could see the look upon Athian's face change, a look of discontent and fear, it was clear for us all to see. With what happened last time we were in paradise we were in no rush to return. But deep down I knew that we had to, I was terrified of returning to the place that I lost my father, not knowing what I was going to find once there. I tried my hardest not to show any of them that I was scared "It will be okay Athian, we'll be there together."

We weren't too sure where we were, so in my head I kept thinking where was paradise from here? We were at sea with no sails and no oars to move us through the water. We sat still on the boat for a while before we noticed in the distance that we could see dark skies. They were the same dark skies that we saw when we were near the wastelands, only this time they were in a south westerly direction. I now knew roughly where we were, we were on the other side of paradise, we were in the eastern seas. Just as we were all thinking that we were completely stranded the boat had started to drift, then suddenly from nowhere the weather started to change. It was no where near the strength of the storm but there was now a breeze in the air and it was pushing the boat, the boat was now able to move in the water, we were moving freely once again, the waves started to form and we were moving steadily along with them. It was nice to know that we weren't totally stranded, only this time we had different concerns, we were moving towards the dark skies that were in the distance.

Return Of The Bloodstone

Chapter 8

The boat was drifting steadily through the waters and we were getting closer to the distant looming darkness. Knowing at some point we were going to reach land and be amongst that darkness itself we decided to use this time to rest and recover the best that we could, we had to prepare for what lay ahead of us.

We had narrowly escaped the cave with our lives and even after resting I was still feeling very fatigued. Sloan was sat at the front of the boat with the chest between his feet. He was constantly reading the markings that were inscribed upon it, trying to understand what they said. He had to make sure he understood all he could before attempting to open and look at a thousand year old gemstone. The inscriptions upon the chest weren't words, they were more like images, ancient symbols all showing what appeared to be a story line. On the front of the chest the images showed the world in a shade of black with it burning in fire and surrounded by demons or monsters. The images to the right showed what appeared to be a battle between demons and common folk. The left side of chest showed a similar image to that on the right side, but this image was clearly showing a battle of magic, warlock against warlock and witch against witch. The image on the back was a strange one, It was an image of what appeared to be the Bloodstone, Only the colouring of it was split. One half of it was a red shade while the other half was pure black, It was a polished black, I'd never seen a black as dark as this. The top of the chest had a written inscription upon it, it was written in the ancient language of the elders, although Sloan could recognise and possibly read and understand the language it's time in the deep sea had caused rust and decay which made it difficult to clearly see. With the salt and rust corroding parts of the wording Sloan couldn't take the risk of a mistake when attempting to read it. I'm sure Sloan was going to attempt to read it at some point, but he didn't want to make any mistakes and have anything unnatural happen. The bottom of the chest had an image that we couldn't see at all. Over time being lost in the salty depths of the sea and the cave the chest had started to rust which distorted the image that was embossed on it's base. "Just open it Sloan, let's have a look at the Bloodstone." "No Athian, not yet and not here." "Why not? We can't take the chest with us everywhere we go." "We must first learn what we must do."

I was thinking the same as Athian, I wanted to see the Bloodstone, to actually look upon what it was that we had all risked our lives to retrieve. I'm sure Krissy would have been wanting to see it also but as she was fast asleep we left her to it. Even with the sound of the waves and the rocking of the boat she still didn't wake.

We drifted on further and the clouds could be seen to be getting closer. Sloan decided that it was time to remove the chains. The chains were not bound with a lock, they appeared to be one continuous length with no joining link. They weren't going to be broken by physical force, but this didn't stop Sloan from trying to break them with brute force. He used all his might to break any link in the chains but he was unable to do so. Athian saw that he was struggling and also attempted to break the chains, both of them twisting and pulling at different parts hoping for any link to break. Even though the chest had been in the salty seas for over a thousand years the chain didn't appear to be corroded, it wasn't going to be broken easily. A silent muttering then came from Krissy as she woke "You might need to try your magic." She was right, if the chest was sealed by magic then that's what was going to open it.

Sloan started to focus hard on the chest and spoke incantation after incantation but the chains still weren't breaking. The chest was locked and it appeared that we had no way of obtaining what was hidden within. We had to think of a way to open it. After feeling frustrated Sloan left the chest at the front of the boat and attempted to sleep. Meanwhile the rest of us sat discussing what had happened in the cave. "I can't believe how you fought against that dragon Krissy." "I can Mickel, just look at her, she's prepared to fight anything." Krissy just giggled and responded "It wasn't easy, but I had to try something." "Well I'm glad you did what you did." "Weren't you scared?" "Terrified Athian, I was terrified." She then went quiet and didn't want to discuss it any further.

While Sloan was sleeping Athian moved the chest closer to himself and using his small hunting knife he started to scrape away some of the rust and residue from the top of the chest. "You won't be able to open it." "I'm cleaning it." I left him to continue in his attempt to scrape away what he could, he wasn't going to stop even if I asked him to. There wasn't much more we could do. Krissy was still tired so she closed her eyes and returned to her sleep, Sloan was now in a deep rest. His snoring reminded me of the noise the hogs made back in the village, hearing this made me think of home again, it made me think of my father, "Athian, I'm going to rest a little, wake us if you see any land."

Meanwhile Blaine had sent all his loyal masters out searching for ancient scribes. These scribes were scattered randomly throughout the world. Each warlock and witch that Blaine sent out searching for scribes had with them city guards and a demon. They went to every village in the south that was either still burning from previous attacks, completely destroyed or that had yet to be attacked. Every village that they went to was completely destroyed before they left them, killing any who got in their way or refused to tell them where the elders were. They left carnage in village after village leaving nothing standing and very few alive. No matter how many villages they went to, they still didn't manage to obtain any scribes.

Davos had the main of the dark legion with him and gathered them all together before the darkness of the night arrived. He placed himself in the centre of the legion and started to speak an ancient incantation. A bright red glow started to appear from his hands and from this a red mist started to spread in to air around him. As it got thicker and thicker it started to enshrouded each of his fighters, it appeared to disappear into them. They were breathing it in, they weren't just taking it into their lungs but it was being absorbed into their skin. Eventually the mist had completely disappeared and they all stood around Davos not knowing what was happening to them. The demons started to let out loud roars. The roaring was so loud and frightening that it brought fear to the city guards that were amongst them. Davos then spoke "You are all now stronger and faster. Once the night has fallen upon us go forth through the swamp and wastelands, every village you come across search for any ancient scribes, kill who you must and destroy what you can."

The sun has started to set and Davos had moved Blaine's dark legion as far north as he could. As the sun got lower and lower in the sky the aggressive roars and shouting from both demons and guards alike could be heard across the whole swamplands. Darkness had fallen upon the lands and the legion had passed through the swamplands with ease and they were now moving through the wastelands, They were widely spread across the wastelands all heading in northerly directions. The sound of the guards steel swords clattering against their armour was deafening as they raced through the dark baron wastelands. Their heavy foot steps pounding into the soil kicking up a dust cloud behind them. The demons had nothing restraining them, they were now much faster than previously and they soon found themselves far ahead of the guards that were trying their hardest to keep up with them.

The magical speed and strength imposed upon them all by Davos allowed them to cross the wastelands in hours rather than days. They soon found themselves encroaching upon the grasslands and started their search for common folk villages. The city guards needed to cross the wastelands fast as the demons that were racing on ahead of them wouldn't be able to physically obtain any knowledge of scribes or to retrieve them. All they knew was to cause death, chaos and destruction to fulfil their blood-lust desires.

In order to control the demons Davos had to port himself to the other side of the wastelands. Having not been there before he was unable to control the exact location of where he would appear. He got lucky with his port and found himself exactly where he wanted to be. The demons had already crossed and he could see the city guards rushing towards him. He instantly started to search for signs of the demons. It didn't take him long before he could hear screams from common folk, screams of horror and fear as the demons were imposing their hatred upon them. He quickly rushed in the direction that he heard the horrors coming from and upon reaching them he could see remains of people that had been either mauled to death or ripped to pieces. The demons had been given instruction by their master to listen to and obey Davos "Cease the killing and come to me" as Davos said this the demons started to cease their attacks upon the common folk and gathered to Davos following the very command that was issued to them. The guards had now crossed the wastelands and also made their way towards to Davos.

The magical spell that was cast upon them had started to fade. For some it had already faded away and they were left straggling behind in the wastelands having to find their own way across with their own abilities. Davos gathered the demons and guards together and told the guards to search the village for the elders. They were ordered not to kill them but to bring them to him.

Any people that were still alive and hiding were pulled from their homes and were forced to their knees in-front of Davos. One by one Davos asked them where the village elder was, but he got little in response. He decided to take a different approach to obtain the information that he was looking for. He approached a woman that was knelt down before him "Where is your elder?" as she failed to reply he reached out his arms and wrapped his hands around her throat, lifting her from her knees and holding her out high above the ground in-front of himself. Again he asked her "Where is your elder?" She was unable to speak as the grip around her throat was so tight that her very life was being choked from her. Davos then let go of the woman and she fell hard to the ground. As she lay on the ground sobbing and in pain she still failed to give a response. Seeing such resilience angered Davos and he called forward one the demons and pointed at the woman "feast." The demon pounced on the woman pinning her to the ground. It opened its jaws wide and sunk it's long blood stained teeth deep into her neck. Closing its jaws hard around her neck and pulling back viscously tearing a large chunk of flesh from her. As she lay dead on the ground with the beast feeding on her flesh. Davos approached the next person, only to find this one was being less defiant and was pleading for their life. "Where is your elder?" After witnessing what had just happened to the woman he didn't hesitate in giving a response. "He's not here, none of them are." "Where are they?" "They might be at the new mountain settlement." Where can I find this new mountain settlement? where?" "Follow the border of the wastelands west, towards the mountains. You will find it there." "See that wasn't too difficult was it?" Davos turned and started to walk away from the man, as he got a few steps away he stopped, turned slightly to his side and pointed at the man "Kill him, kill them all" As he said this the demon that was feasting on it's earlier kill pounced on the man and started to tear him limb from limb. The city guards walked forward and started to slaughter all the other people that remained alive. Screams of pain and suffering could be heard as the guards lunged their swords deep into their victims bodies or slicing them multiple times before eventually slitting their throats. Once they had killed all in the village they started their march west following the borders of the wastelands and heading towards the south side of the mountains.

Back in the eastern seas they were now all awake. They couldn't see clearly where the boat was drifting them towards but they knew from the night stars above them that they were heading in a westerly direction. Athian had finished cleaning up the old chest to the best that he could. He managed to remove most of the debris and made the ancient language inscribed upon it more visual. Sloan didn't appear to be in any rushed attempt to translate the inscription, he was more focussed on looking out to dark seas wondering where they were venturing towards. "Sloan, I've clean the chest up for you." "Thank you Athian," Sloan didn't appear to be enthusiastic about what Athian had just told him. "You can now read it Sloan, the writing is now clearly visible. You should be able to read what it says." With Athian explaining more in what he had done Sloan this time showed more attention to what Athian had said and with more enthusiasm he pulled the chest closer towards himself. He then leaned out of the boat and cupped water from the sea into his hands, he let the water flow over the chest and started to remove the dust from the top of it. The inscriptions had now become darker and easier to read. "Athian come here and conjure me your light orb." Athian moved across the boat and sat right beside Sloan. He slowly conjured his light once more. I was quite impressed, he was getting very good at this type of magic, for him it is a great achievement for someone like Sloan or Gideon I would imagine that it's very basic. "That's bright enough." Sloan focussed hard on the writing and started to read it quietly to himself. He read it twice to ensure himself that he didn't make any mistakes in translation. I sat focussing on him and noticed a confused look come across his face. I decided to ask him what it says. "It's confusing Mickel. It has two meanings, what they completely mean I don't understand." "Can you not open it?" asked Krissy. "I'm not sure how." replied Sloan. Athian usually always has some sort of verbal opinion on such things "Just read it out loud, it seems to work with other magic that was in the book." Sloan looked at Athian "You try it." Athian pulled the chest closer to himself and attempted to read the writing on the chest. His attempt was pretty terrible, Krissy and myself were laughing at the constant stammering and stuttering as he tried to pronounce the words "It's not funny." He tried to read it again and yet again he was still unable to pronounce the word's correctly. Sloan had heard enough and snatched the chest away from Athian. "Oh give it here." He started to read the old language fluently and as smoothly as he could. He was speaking loud and clear making sure that he didn't pronounce anything wrong. Once he had finished that's when we noticed the chest started to glow a bright red, it was glowing as bright as it was when he first saw it. A light was illuminating from inside of the chest, the chains had started to turn to a dark orange and they appeared to be getting hot. The chains got so hot that the links had started to distort and weaken, the chain links were melting. It only took a few minutes and the chains had completely melted away. Although the chest could now be opened the melting steel links had caused another issue. They had started to burn through the boat, the red hot steel was burning into the deck of the boat creating holes and damaging our only form of a safe haven. Seeing this Sloan quickly cast a spell upon the hot melted steel which saw it cool fast and set quickly, luckily the cooling steel was able to block most the holes that it had just created.

Once Sloan had repaired the damage caused by the molten steel we all started to focus once again on the chest. The chains were now gone and the bright red light that had been glowing from inside was now near nothing more than a flicker. Sloan placed his hands on either side of the chest and slowly started to lift the lid open. The lid appeared to be stuck, It was difficult for Sloan to open so he added a bit more force to it and attempted to open it a second time. We were all watching cautiously, eager to see what the Bloodstone looked like, that's if there was one in the chest.

Hi second attempt was successful, he had broke the thousand year old seal, he slowly started to open the chest, the creaking sound that came from the chest as the lid was opened sent shivers through my body. I was expecting to see water or slime from the sea come from the chest as it was opened but that wasn't the case. Instead what came out of it was a burst of thick brown dust which made us all start to cough as it filled the air we were breathing in. After several minutes the dust had cleared and we were all able to breathe easily once again. The top of the chest was now completely open, we peered into the chest hoping to see the Bloodstone, but what we saw was part of an animal hide, an animal hide which was wrapped around an item. Sloan slowly put his hands into the chest and withdrew what lay within. He lay the animal hide carefully across the deck of the boat, he then slowly started to unravel it, being careful not to allow what was wrapped within it to roll and fall from the boat. He peeled back the hide wrapping, revealing one side at a time until the item was completely revealed.

There it was, the Bloodstone had been found. It was no bigger than the size of an egg, it wasn't round and smooth like the pearl but it had an eye catching appearance. It looked like an egg with scales. The inner part of the scales had different shades of red while the outer edges were black. Although it was one stone it looked like it was formed by multiple sections. The centre of each section peace was flickering with a red glow, It was as if it was alive, the red glow was shining and dimming in a steady rhythm, a rhythm like a beating heart. We all sat staring at it with none of us willing to pick it up.

Return Of The Bloodstone

Krissy was particularly drawn to it's shine and appearance. She moved herself closer to the Bloodstone and slowly reached her hand across to touch it. As she did this the red glow that was illuminating from the stone appeared to fade. "That's strange" as she saw this she moved her hand away and the glow reappeared. Athian then wanted to try "Let me try it" The effect was the same. It appeared that the Bloodstone was sensing any attempt made to touch it. Sloan decided that maybe he should try. He didn't hesitate or take his time, he put his hand across the top of it and picked it straight up, the red glow didn't fade at all, if anything it appeared to glow brighter. He put both hands around it and gripped it as firmly as he could. It started to glow brighter and brighter, the red light that was shining from it was now so bright that it was hurting our eyes, all the black patches we saw on it had completely faded, it was now completely red. With the Bloodstone firmly in his grasp Sloan spoke "I am the holder."

It was just as Sloan had told us, there can be only one holder and the holder could not make the decision. So no we had to figure out who the decision maker was, the elder told us that Mickel had a decision to make but that could have been for anything. Sloan was about to put the Bloodstone back into the hide and this is when he noticed writing inscribed on the inside of the animal hide. It appeared to be written in blood. What type of blood it was we didn't stop to think about, but as none of us could read the ancient text Sloan translated it for us. "The holder cannot decide, they are merely to abide. One to decide for all or to decide for the one. Once the decision is made, the choice cannot be undone." I listened intently to what Sloan had just read out to us "It's a riddle" A sigh could be heard from Athian before he spoke "Another riddle, we struggled with the last one, how do we solve this one."

I knew the riddle was a choice that had to be made. It was clear that Sloan was the holder and he was to have no say in any decision of the Bloodstone's use. But the decision of what had to be done is what we needed to think about and we currently had plenty of time to think. Sloan put the stone back into the animal hide and wrapped it up tightly before then placing it into his holding satchel. We had all been so focussed on the Bloodstone that none of us had realised where we had drifted to. Krissy was the first to notice "Look I see land" and rest assured there it was, land was directly in front us. It was a cliff face, as far as we could see, there was a tall black rocked cliff face. Below it there was a long narrow sandy beach and directly above all of it was a thick black cloud. Now we had to work out where we were and where we had to go from here.

Chapter 9

Davos had marched his army right across the south side of the Argian Valley heading towards the mountains and the new settlement. They had passed through several villages on their westward trek and they ensured that they left no structures standing and no one alive. The trail of death and destruction was a long and bloodied one. Davos knew that they didn't have much time as sunrise would soon be upon them. He had to ensure that he found a daylight sanctuary, somewhere for the demons to safely stay and he had to find one soon.

They had marched so far west that they could soon see the mountains before them. But that wasn't the only thing they saw, they could also see what appeared to be a fortified settlement. Davos kept the legion marching close enough to the settlement so that they were in attacking range. He gathered the army together and told them that they were not to destroy any structures and that they were to keep any important people in the settlement alive. He called forth one of the city guards "Jax, come forth." A large city guard appeared before him. "I must go and return with our master, you are to take control here. The demons will come with me and we shall return when the sun sets. Do as I have ordered, do not destroy the structures and do not kill anyone, wait for my return." "Yes my lord, I shall heed your instructions."

Davos called all the demons to his side and opened a portal for them to travel through. He opened the portal just in time as behind him to the east the sun had started to rise. He ordered them all through before following them through it himself. Just as the portal closed the darkness of the night had faded and the lands were now lit up with the brightness of a fresh new day.

Davos appeared back in paradise before his master "Why are you back here and not with the legion? Where are the scrolls?" Davos hesitated before speaking "We haven't found any scrolls yet master, but we have moved north of the wastelands and we will soon find the elders and the ancient scrolls." "You are now north of the wastelands? "Yes master Blaine." Where is the unholy legion." "They are safe, I brought them here to paradise master. I have left Jax in control of the city guards, they are remaining in the north awaiting my return. They are preparing for battle which I'm sure will lead us to the scrolls you seek."

Blaine was furious with the news that no scrolls had yet been found, he demanded that Davos take him to the guards. "You will take me to the guards now." "But master what about the unholy? the north is now in sunlight."

Return Of The Bloodstone

"They will remain here for now, take me to my army." Blaine and Davos used their magical abilities and were soon stood with the guards. When they appeared at the encampment they saw that the army was ready for battle.

Jax had them all prepared and ready to attack the settlement, they were ready for war. Blaine stood staring at the mountain settlement "Well, what are you waiting for, get me my scrolls." Jax then gave the order for the army to attack. The front line didn't rush towards the settlement but they walked in a disciplined line. As they advanced towards the settlement walls screams could be heard coming from the other-side. The common folk that were left behind to protect the settlement soon made themselves visual. They were armed and were stood along the basic defensive wall with archers and swordsman waiting on the inside. As the city guards marched closer and closer to them they launched a volley of arrows down towards them. The whistling sound made by the arrows as they sliced through the air could be heard by all. The first volley of arrows that were fired towards them all fell short or their target. They waited a minute longer, relocked their bows and launched a second volley of arrows against the oncoming legion. They looked on as the arrows started to descend and saw that this time they were on target. The arrows all came down at once but Blaine's city guards didn't appear fazed by them. They continued to advance towards the basic defensive wall that was before them. The arrows came crashing down upon them but had little if no effect.

The armour of the guards was too strong, the arrows either deflected off of them or snapped upon impact. Seeing this the common folk started to panic "Start the fires, quickly get the fire wall burning." The Archers this time aimed flamed arrows at the ground. As the arrows hit the ground they ignited an oil which had been poured into the soil. A large fire wall had formed in front of the settlement. They had remembered what they were told about fire defeating demons, only what they didn't know was that the advancing threat towards them were men and warlock.

The guards eventually got to the fire wall and stopped their march forward. Suddenly they all parted and created a gap in their front line. Blaine and Davos walked through the gap and extinguished the wall of fire, the flames were quickly reduced to nothing and then attacked the barrier with magic. Davos was looking up to the skies and started to speak a spell, clouds then formed above him and strong winds started to blow fiercely against the village defences, lighting started to strike down and set fire to the wooden barriers. Blaine thrust his hands forward and parts of the wall were torn apart. The city guards then rushed through the defensive lines and into the settlement.

The common folk that were waiting on the other side of the wall were no match for the fully armoured and skilled fighters that they were about to encounter. Although they tried to defend themselves they were soon overpowered. With their large razor sharp swords the guards sliced through them as if they weren't even there.

Those that were further back in the village saw what was happening to their men and fled towards the mine entrances. Taking with them any children or elderly that were able to move. Many fell during the scramble to safety and were injured as they were crushed or trampled by others rushing to safety.

The settlement defences were all burning, the centre of the settlement was now crowded with common folk that hadn't managed to escape. The guards had rounded them all up and forced them all to their knees. They had them all lined up before Blaine and Davos. Jax was stood behind the first man "Who is your elder?" the man failed to reply. He wasn't asked a second time, Jax pulled his sword from his sheaf and with one swing decapitated the man. The man's body fell to the ground as his bloodied head rolled past the others that were beside him. The blood that was flowing freely from the man's decapitated body was being absorbed by the ground. The second man in the line attempted to escape, he tried to run but he was no match for Jax. He quickly grabbed the man by his hair and pulled him to the ground hard. He leaned over the man wrapped his hands around his neck and then lifted him high off the ground. He clenched his hands so tightly around the man's neck that he couldn't breathe, blood started to appear in the man's eyes and then it started to drip from the sides of his mouth. With one twist of his hands a snapping sound could be heard, the man was dead. Jax dropped the body to the ground like it was nothing more than a cloth rag, again the ground around them appeared to absorb the blood that was now dripping from the new corpse. "Who's next to die? Tell my masters what they want to know." No one replied, they were all being quiet, they were remaining silent for a reason, they were stalling the evil that had fallen upon them. They were giving the other's time to escape, time to get deep into the mines, they were sacrificing themselves. "If none of you speak then you will all die, then so will those running to the mountain." The men started to look at each other and they were all thinking the same thing, they were all thinking to say nothing.

Blaine walked forward and stood before them, his eyes were glowing red and the black veins down the side of his head and neck were pulsating heavily. He was stood directly in-front of one man, he reached out his arm and forced him to his feet. He put his hand out and placed it on the man's forehead. The man's eyes started to move rapidly before they suddenly turned a solid black. Blaine was in his head, searching for information that he required. The man started to shake vigorously then suddenly spoke "Mickel, Sloan, these are my elders." Blaine kept his hand on the man a little while longer and the man again spoke "The book of magic, I need to protect the it." Blaine removed his hand from the man's forehead and walked away, "Kill them all, and find me this book of magic."

Jax quickly drew his sword out again and within seconds

he had sliced through the remaining men that were kneeling on the ground around him. He was brutal with his killing, all the swings of his sword found their target's with ease and didn't appear to miss. The rest of the city guards started to search through all the structures that they could enter. One of them then appeared before Davos holding something in his hands. "Davos, I have found this." He handed Davos a small satchel, he opened the satchel and inside he saw a book, an old book, it was the book of magic. "Master, we have the book." Blaine took the book and started to look through it's pages. He noticed that there were some pages throughout the book that were blank. There was no writing on them just a small wax seal stamped into the corners. Blaine then started to walk through the settlement looking for anything that might lead him towards the scrolls. He wasn't able to find anything else of interest to him. He walked towards the mountain and stood still staring at it. "What are you looking at master?" "A new fortitude Davos, a constant darkness, a place to bring forth all that I require. A new start to my dark world." "Here Master, why here?" "Did you not witness the ground absorbing the blood?" "Yes, I thought that was you." "No it wasn't me, but it was a sign, a sign that the lands here are dark, a darkness that wants to grow. So we will feed it what it wants" Davos then walked back to the village grounds where Jax had earlier slaughtered the villagers, he started to look at ground around him and noticed that all the corpses were completely drained of blood, all the blood that had flowed from these corpses had been completely absorbed into the ground. He then started to look around the settlement, all the green grass that was here had wilted away to weeds, the trees leaves were starting to fall as if they were going through a seasonal change. Blaine was right, this is the area in which he was to summon his army and take control of the world.

Davos called Jax forward and ordered him to take the army into the mountains, "Go and find those that escaped and return here with them. Once you have them back here in the settlement kill them all, ensure that you spill all their blood here." Blaine had the book of magic in his hands and had started to read through it. Most of what he was reading from the book he already knew but there were some spells which were new to him, some spells which would make him stronger. He was looking for some particular information, spells or incantations that would help him rule the world. He was looking for dark elemental spells, but more specifically he was looking for a spell that would allow him to black out the sun. He wanted the world to be dark, he wanted it to be a forever night. He knew that as long as the sun could shine onto the lands then he would struggle to develop his new world of darkness.

He ordered Davos to remain here with the city guards and to make sure that he cleansed the mountains and all the surrounding areas of any common folk or tribes. With his staff in his hand he used a different magic spell, instead of calling forth a travelling portal he started to read a spell from the book which saw him change to a black mist and then suddenly disappear from sight.

Blaine soon found himself back in the temple hall, he called forth all his dark legion and commanded them to remain in the darkness with him. He started to study the book in more depth. While doing this he noticed that some of the pages were completely free from dust. He waved his hand across these pages before speaking "Show me what was sought." The book pages suddenly started to turn on their own. They were rapidly being turned, page after page before stopping on a specific one. The page that it stopped on was the one that Sloan was reading, the page with knowledge of the Bloodstone. Blaine started to read the page and he now knew what was being sought and why it was being sought. He continued to look through the book and started to focus on the blank pages. "Show me what is hidden" nothing appeared "Reveal to me all that is lost" but still no words appeared on the pages, they were still blank. As nothing appeared on the pages Blaine started to get frustrated and angry. He clenched his fists so tightly that his nails sunk deep into his palms causing them to bleed. The dark red blood dripped from his hand and onto the pages, his blood was so dark that it was nearly black.

As Blaine saw his own blood dripping onto the pages and he attempted to wipe it away, as his hand was still bleeding from the wound all he had actually done was to make the blood on the pages worse. In frustration he attempted to wipe it away again but it smeared across the books blank pages "Damn it" He then decided to wipe it away with part of his robe and that's when he noticed the pages had changed, writing and scriptures had now appeared on the blank pages. His blood had revealed what was written and hidden on them. Now knowing how to reveal what could not be seen Blaine used his magic and pulled to himself one of the city guards. He commanded the guard to stand over the book. The guard placed the book beneath him and was stood directly over it. Before the guard knew it Blaine had pulled a dagger from his belt and sliced the guards throat open from ear to ear. Blood was flowing fast and freely from the guard, dripping down and covering the whole book. Blaine held the guard over the book and ensured that no part of it was left untarnished. Once the book was covered in enough blood he tossed the body of the guard to one side and told his hounds to feast. He picked up the book of magic and started to wipe away the excess blood that had flowed upon it. As he started to turn the pages he could now see that none of them were blank, They all now had writing upon them, he had unlocked the books hidden secrets.

He sat back in his throne and started to read through it again, only this time there was much more for him to obtain from it, more secrets revealed, more power for him to gain. After a few hours of searching the south side of the mountains Jax whom had recently been appointed legion general by Davos returned with dozens of men, women and children that had earlier escaped. He walked them all to the centre of the settlement. They all had their hands bound behind their backs and were unable to defend themselves. Jax spaced them all around ten paces apart from each-other and one by one he started to slice their throats. Screams of terror and fear from all the onlooking common folk echoed through the south side of the mountains. Body after body, they all hit the ground hard and their blood was quickly absorbed into it as it poured from the open wounds.

With this brutal killing of innocent people the ground was puddled in their blood. But it didn't stay there for long, it was all soon absorbed by the dark soil and all the land around it was changing, It was changing the whole area, any green plant life that was in the village soon wilted away. The soil started to turn black and the trees looked more like giant bare branches rather than the once flourishing life that they once were. Daylight was still amongst them and Davos ordered Jax to take the guards and set up camp at the base of the mountain. "Nightfall will soon be here, we need to have base camp set up quickly, tomorrow we take the northern villages. These lands need to be soaked in blood" Loud cheers could be heard to be coming from the guards as they quickly went about setting up camp for the night. Blaine had continued to read through the book of magic hoping that he would find what he was looking for. He had managed to obtain some knowledge of what was required to change the world and this involved the Bloodstone. All he had to do now was to wait, wait for Mickel and the others to bring it to him.

Return Of The Bloodstone

Chapter 10

We stood facing what was going to be a very physically task ahead of us. The black cliffs that were before us were tall and appeared to have no easy way of climbing them. We couldn't go backwards so we had no choice, the cliff had to be climbed. We all walked along the base of the cliff face looking for anywhere that appeared to be suitable for climbing. We had no climbing spikes and no ropes with us so we had to be sure that we found the safest route.

We slowly moved along the sandy beach trying to find any place along this wall of rock that we could use to our benefit. It took a while but we found an area with what appeared to be a ledge, a ledge that we would be able to climb. The only problem was that the starting point of this ledge was a good height up from the cliff base. I could see a tree growing out from the side of the cliff. Athian had also spotted the same tree that I had "If we could climb to that tree then we would be closer to the ledge" I had to agree with Athian "But how do we get to the tree?" Krissy walked to the face of the cliff and took out two of her daggers. With her left hand she stabbed her dagger into the cliff face. She pulled herself up the wall and did the same with her right hand. She was doing it, she was pulling herself up the wall and making her way towards the tree. She repeated the same process with her left hand again, piercing deep into the rock face that she was now ascending. As she did this again with her right hand it didn't seem to pierce the rock wall deep enough. She tried again and this time the blade appeared to enter the rock deeper but it still wasn't fully secure. She still attempted to pull herself upwards, as she pulled herself up with her right arm and swung her left arm up she suddenly fell to beach that was below. The dagger had gave way and her body hit the ground hard. She lay on the beach rolling in agonising pain. Mickel ran across to her as quickly as he could, he wanted to ensure that she was okay. She was badly bruised but there were no serious injuries noticeable.

"Great we're never going to get up this cliff" "Not now Athian" Over the last year Sloan had learnt a lot about Athian and one of the things that he had learnt was that he looks on the negative side of things too much. He has to keep giving him reminders to hush up at times. We sat in the sand and we had to come up with a way to climb to that tree. "Can we not magic up some steps" "No Athian, we can't" Mickel asked Sloan if he could create a portal to get us off of the beach and up the cliff. "Sorry Mickel, It's too risky. I don't have full control of where it would take us. We could end up nowhere near where we need to be."

We couldn't stay here on the beach and do nothing, we had to find a way up this cliff face. There had to be somewhere that was accessible for us. We walked back towards the edge of the water so we could obtain a clearer view. Nothing before us looked like a good safe area. We walked along the water's edge looking at the face of this giant wall before us. Yet we still couldn't see any area that was safe to climb. Krissy was walking slowly behind us, she appeared to be in discomfort from her fall. Sloan knew that he had to do something but wasn't sure what he could do to help. A portal was the obvious decision but he knew that it was too risky. After walking along the beach for a while longer they were all thinking that maybe they should just go back to the boat and try to drift further down the seas but what difference would that make? They would still only see what they are seeing now, a wall of rock before them and vast seas behind them stuck in a dark covered land.

The beach area started to get smaller and smaller. The further we walked the sand got wetter and firmer under our feet. The seas were closing in on the rock wall, the tide was coming in. Now we desperately needed to climb this wall no matter what the risk was. "The tides coming in, Sloan we need to get up this cliff." we were now walking directly at the base of the cliff. The boat was no longer in sight and the tide had reached the cliff face behind us. The waves were getting strong and they had started to crash against the wall of rock.

We eventually came to part of the cliff that appeared to have an opening in it, we had found a keyhole. Most keyhole entrances are easy to notice but this wasn't very large, but it was big enough to give us entrance. "Not another cave" muttered Athian. "We have to enter, we can't stay out here." Sloan was right. This was our way off of the beach. We had no choice. We couldn't climb the cliff and the tide behind us was coming in too quickly.

Cave entrances can be deceiving, some may appear to be small at the entrance but inside they could be vast and have many passageways to follow. One by one we entered the caves keyhole. Sloan was the first to enter followed by Athian, I made sure that Krissy got through safely before entering myself. Once we were all inside we couldn't see anything. It was blacker than night. There was no light in here at all. "Athian do your thing." He actually listened to me and he managed to call forth his light orb. It gave us enough light for what we needed. We had to walk crouched down for a short while but the further we walked the more open space we suddenly found.

We could taste the salt on our lips and feel it drying on our skin. Soon the shallow water that was below our feet had disappeared and we walking on solid rock. Eventually the rocks that we were walking on were dry. Although we were in a cave we knew that with no water beneath our feet and on dry rock then we were ascending. The passage that we were on was leading us through the cave and upwards, it was leading us up to the top of the cliff.

We had moved quite a way through the cave and the salty taste that was upon our lips had started to fade. However the air was becoming harder to breathe. It was getting thicker and we were struggling to move at a quick pace. We decided to stop and rest for a little while. Athian was struggling to maintain the light so he closed his incantation. We all sat in darkness while we gained back a little of our strength. We didn't have much food or water left so we rationed what we had.

148

Return Of The Bloodstone

After a short while we started following the passage once again. Athian didn't use any of his magic this time, but Sloan did. As Sloan's magic was too far beyond Athian to apprehend, he found it much easier to call forth a light orb. The light given off was so much brighter than what my good friend could create. We could see a lot further down the passage of the cave. As we were moving further inwards and upwards we all thought we heard something move. "What the heck was that" "Nothing Athian, it was nothing" I know that Sloan was only trying to reassure Athian as I heard it also. Something was in here with us. Something was moving in the darkness keeping itself out of sight and hidden in the shadows. We continued walking through the cave and then again we heard a noise, it came from in-front of us. This time it was clear enough for us all to hear. It was the sound of rocks sliding, as if they were falling from above, something was definitely in these caves with us.

"See, I told you I heard something, maybe we should stop" "We need to keep going Athian, we can't just stop. We need to get out of here before the air runs out." "Okay, Let's just get out of here fast then." We started to pick up our walking pace, whatever it was that was in here with us was moving in the same direction as ourselves but it was staying ahead of the light. We came to a split in the passage, one passageway kept us going straight on, continuing on a steady ascending path while the other passageway broke off leading to the left. It didn't appear to ascend or descend it just seemed to continue on the same level. Which way to follow we all had to decide together. We stopped for a short while to ensure we all came to the same decision. After a short discussion we decided to take the passageway that was leading us upwards. After all it was the top of the cliff that we wanted to get to.

The salt in the air had now nearly cleared, this was a good sign, a sign that we were getting higher. Our only concerns were the current air level in the cave and whatever it was that was moving in-front of us. We must of walked for another thirty minutes or so and we didn't even realise it at the time but the air was easier to breathe, now we had only the one concern.

We took the fact that air coming into the cave was a good sign, we had taken the correct passage. As we continued walking we again heard a sound coming from in-front of us, it sounded like rocks falling once more. "Quickly let's go and see what it is." Krissy marched on past us walking ahead of the light, she was wanting to find out what it was that we were unknowingly following. We all picked up our pace to make sure that we didn't lose sight of her. She must of felt much better now after her previous fall as we were struggling to keep up. We came to an open area in the cave but it didn't look like it was part of the cave, it looked more like a stone room.

Looking around where we had found ourselves we couldn't see anyone or find anything here. We definitely followed the sounds that were coming from in-front of us. There didn't appear to be any openings or exit points in this room. Sloan started to walk around the room moving the light orb with him, casting lights into the darkness. He moved around the room as slowly as he could and when he got to one part of the room we all heard an almighty screech, a screech that came from something else, something that was in here with us. We then heard something scurrying across the stone floor. What it was we still didn't know. Sloan knew that whatever it was that was in here it feared the light. He decided to stop the spell that was giving us clear sight so he could flush out whatever it was that was hiding in the shadows.

As the light dwindled we all suddenly heard more movement from within this stone room. It wasn't only movement that we heard, but we also heard what sounded like a low deep rumbling growl. We all kept as close as we could to each-other, trying our best to keep sight of each other and away from the noises. With the room now being in complete darkness we struggled to see. Krissy came up with an idea which seemed to be a safe one "Grab each-others arms, this way we won't get separated." The three of us grabbed hold to each-other while Sloan was slowly walking around the room. He was moving towards the growling and movement sounds. As the room was in complete darkness the low quiet growl had now become a loud aggressive roar. We kept close together and moved ourselves back against one of the cold wet walls. We then heard what sounded like rushing feet across the ground, something was coming towards us and it was moving fast. Whatever it was that was in here with us it was getting closer and closer. And just as it was in-front of us a large fireball came from one side of the room. The fireball struck the beast hard and it fell to the ground before us, we moved away from it as it burst into flames. It was rolling around and screaming in pain. "What the hell is that thing?"

Screaming and dying on the stone floor in-front of us was a small night demon. It's a hairless demon which has no eyes, Its mouth is wide and full of razor sharp teeth. It had multiple layers of them, teeth behind teeth all which looked like they could rip through flesh with ease. Its nails were more like claws. They were all long and curved with each one of them leading to a sharp point that could possibly pierce through armour. Sloan walked forward from out of the darkness and stood over the burning body "This is a night demon" "Oh my god it stinks," "Is it dead Sloan?" "It's dying, these things don't like sunlight or fire, that's their weakness." Using the light from the burning night demons corpse Sloan started to look around the stone room, he was trying to find an alternative exit. He knew that with the night demon being down in these passageways that there had to be another way into them.

After looking around the room he found what appeared to be a small opening. Once Sloan had finished looking over the opening he called the others across to him. "We need to go through here, hopefully this will lead us up and out of here."

One by one we each crawled through the opening in the stone wall, Krissy was the last one to go through and just as she managed to pull herself through the opening the light from the burning corpse behind her had completely burnt out. They were now all in a different part of the cave. This section wasn't in complete darkness, the walls here had what appeared to be light reflecting from them. They were not a solid stone but were more like a composite of precious minerals and rock combined. The minerals that were within the rock were creating a sparkle and with thousands upon thousands of them built into the passageway the sparkling from the walls gave off what appeared to be a lightly lit passageway.

We followed the passageway as quietly as we could, keeping an eye out for anything else that may want to cause us harm. The air was still clear enough for us to breathe and we were still ascending. We all knew that at some point the passageway was going to come to end, but where it was leading us to we didn't know. We kept faith in ourselves knowing that we had each-other to rely on.

We eventually came to a wider part of the passage and decided to sit for a while. "Is the Bloodstone still safe Sloan?" Sloan opened his pouch, took out the animal hide and slowly opened it. Once it was opened the Bloodstone was there for us all to see. "Yes it's still safe Mickel" Although it had been wrapped in the animal hide and tucked away safely in Sloan's side pouch it appeared to of taken a different appearance about it, it looked slightly different than what it did before. The red sections appeared to be getting brighter, not as bright as it was when Sloan was holding it, but brighter than it was when we first saw it. It sounds crazy, but it appeared to look like the stone was breathing, I had to rub my eyes as I couldn't believe what I was seeing. I asked Sloan if I could hold it "Of course you can, but not for long as we have to get moving" I picked up the stone and held it in the palm of my hand. I felt a warmth coming from the stone, It still appeared to look like it was breathing, it must have been my eyes. Maybe I just needed a good rest.

As I was holding the Bloodstone I started to feel more relaxed about everything. I was no longer thinking about the bad things that had happened to us. The bad thoughts and memories appeared to be drifting from my mind. All the dark and evil things that I've kept hidden in my mind were fading from my thoughts. I was starting to feel light headed, like my brain was being completely starved of oxygen. As I was feeling this way I looked down to my hand and I saw that the red sections of the Bloodstone had started to turn a dark red, small black patches had also appeared. I didn't just notice the stone pulsating but I could feel it, it appeared again to be beating like a heart, like it was alive. I wasn't sure what was happening, then suddenly the stone was snatched from the palm of my hand "You've held it long enough" Sloan had taken the stone from my hand and wrapped it back into its parchment. "What just happened" I asked as Sloan was putting the Bloodstone safely into his holding pouch. He looked directly up at me before speaking "The Bloodstone's magic had started to work. It was absorbing darkness around it and It had started to absorb the dark thoughts from your mind." Athian and Krissy were looking on and heard what Sloan had said. "You mean it actually absorbs evil and darkness?" "Yes Athian, and we don't need it to absorb any darkness yet."

We didn't completely understand why Sloan didn't want the Bloodstone to absorb any darkness or evil now so Krissy decided to ask him, she wanted more clarification and a little more understanding "Why don't you want it absorbing evil now? Wouldn't it be safer if evil around us was absorbed and away from us?" To me it seemed to make sense what Krissy was asking. Surely with less evil around us it would be safer for us to continue on our journey. I still wasn't completely assured by what Sloan had told us so i decided to speak "If it absorbs darkness and evil then let's keep the stone out, let it draw the evil into it." Sloan looked over at me and I could see in his eyes that he didn't want to continue explaining to us. "Please just trust me." As I could see he was getting angry I didn't mention anything else on the subject, neither did any of the others.

We had rested long enough and we continued walking along the passageway. The wall's of the cave were still giving off it's reflective light. Giving us clear sight of what was ahead of us and around us. The passage soon started to lose it's natural cavern look and started to appear more like man-made stone walls. The minerals that were within the stone structure had started to disappear and the light that they generated had started to diminish. We continued to follow the passage the best we could. Before we knew it we were walking in what appeared to be a narrow brick corridor. We followed it all the way to the end until we could go no further.

We soon found ourselves standing before a steel grated door. On the other-side of this door we could see a large stone stairwell. We all remembered seeing such a similar stairway before, only this time we weren't in the temple, well at-least we didn't think we were. The gate didn't seem to have any chains securing it and there wasn't a key or lock that we had to use in order to open it. Athian grabbed the handle and tried to push open the gate, but the handle wouldn't turn and the gate wouldn't move. "Here let me try it" even after Krissy had tried the handle of the gate it still wouldn't open. Only one of us knew why the door wouldn't open, "The gate is sealed with magic and only magic will open it." As Sloan said this we all stood and looked at him, we were waiting for him to use an incantation but he didn't use one. "Go on then Sloan, open it" Sloan wasn't sure if he should open the gate or not. He knew that the night demon had come from somewhere, but where it came from he didn't know. He knew that it either came from behind them or from the other side of this gate.

As he was stood deciding what to do we all heard movement from behind us. Something was coming our way, we could hear the scurrying of feet moving its way closer and closer and then we heard the growling. It wasn't the growling of one thing but possibly many. It was the same type of growl that we had heard earlier, night demons were heading our way. "Hurry Sloan, open the gate there's something coming for us." Sloan could now hear the growling and the sound of heavy footsteps rushing towards them. He quickly started to speak and incantation to open the gate but the one he used didn't work. He tried a different incantation but again it didn't appear to work on the locked gate. He was trying his hardest to concentrate and to unlock the magical bind that was cast upon the gate.

Krissy took up a fighting stance as she knew the beasts were drawing down upon them. Sloan then shouted out "The spells that I am using are not strong enough, this has been sealed by a warlock stronger than myself." How we were going to get through this gate I didn't know. Krissy then yelled "Hurry, I can see them, they are nearly here." The first beast was now rushing towards Krissy. The corridor wasn't very wide and she used this to her advantage as the beast came rushing towards her. It leapt through the air with its jaws open wide aiming to sink it's teeth deep into it's target. Krissy kept herself low slightly rushing forward and slid under the beast. As she did this she raised her hands up high and her daggers sunk deep into the chest of the beast that was above her. With the beasts momentum and hers combined her daggers sliced deep through the demons chest and down into its stomach. As the beast was brutally opened up Krissy found herself being covered in blood and guts. There was so much blood over her face that she could barely see. She soon found her way back to the others and told them that they needed to hurry and open the gate.

Suddenly I heard Athian speaking the same incantation that Sloan had earlier tried. He couldn't stand and do nothing so he decided to try and open the gate. "What are you doing Athian, if Sloan can't do it then how are you going to?" "I have to help somehow" Although he didn't know it at the time, he was was right. Sloan started to speak the incantation again only this time he was speaking it along with Athian. With the pair of them now speaking the same incantation the combined magic was stronger. It was now stronger than that of the warlock that had cast the locking incantation. A blue light had started to appear around the gates handle and then a clunking sound could be heard. The magic gate had been opened.

The beasts were now insight and were moving their way down the corridor towards them. They all rushed through the gate and made their way towards the stone steps. They rushed up the steps as quickly as they could with the night demons not far behind them. They got to the top of the steps and found a wooden door before them. The door was old and heavy and as such it was difficult to open. With all of their might together they pushed the door open. As it opened they all fell out on to the ground that was on the other-side.

As they lay on the ground several of the night demons had also jumped out through the doorway. They were helpless to do anything as they lay there waiting for what seemed to be a perilous situation for them all. As the demons came through the door and were in the air descending above them they suddenly started to scream in agony. They couldn't believe how lucky they were. For where they had fallen was lit up with light. It was daylight, the sun was shining down upon them. The night demons that rushed through the door following them couldn't stop themselves in time and as the rays of sunlight hit them they caught fire before turning to dust. We all lay there relieved with what had just happened. The dust and debris from the demon corpses showered down upon us. We could see other demons stood in the doorway growling loudly towards us. They then turned and headed back to where they had came from.

We all got up to our feet and dusted ourselves off. Krissy struggled to clean herself down completely as she was covered in blood, guts and now dust. I could tell from the look on her face that she was disgusted and just wanted to get cleaned up. We started to look around the area to see where we were, We all recognised our surroundings, we were back in the city, we were in the arena.

Chapter 11

Back at the settlement not everything seemed to be going to plan for Davos and the city guards. "Davos, we have had intruder's in the camp." Jax was stomping around the camp in a rage waking up as many of his legion as he could. Davos came rushing from his tent to see what was happening "What's all this commotion and shouting about?" He approached Jax who was now in a calmer disposition than earlier, "Someone's been in the camp" He walked Davos across the settlement to where his guards were positioned and pointed them out to him, their bodies were dumped in a pile on top of each-other. "When did this happen? How did this happen?"

During the night while the city guards were standing guard or resting something had entered their encampment and killed several of the guards that were on watch duty along with several that were sleeping. The bodies were just like those of the common folk that they had brutally slaughtered. Their blood was totally drained and absorbed into the land. "You need to find who is responsible for this." Jax started to search the area looking for anything that would give him an insight as to what happened. After searching the bodies he saw from the wounds that they were killed by a thick bladed weapon and a large impact weapon. He found trails of wide foot prints that were leading towards the mine entrances. They weren't foot prints of a beast or animal but were made by men, and judging by the depth of the footprints they were heavy men. Whatever or whomever made them went into the mountains.

He reported his findings to Davos and awaited his next instruction. "So it appears that we are not alone in this area, these lands need to be cleansed. Take some of your legion and flush out whatever it is within the mountain. Kill all you come across." Jax returned to the base of the mountain with a dozen of his finest guards and then gave them all the same instruction, "We enter these mines, we search these mines and we cleanse these mines. Kill all and everything that you come across." They wrapped several branches in oil soaked cloth and set fire to them, they had to ensure that they had light once they were in the mines. The mines were wide but they were not very high. As with most of the guards being tall they all had to squat a little in order to enter the mines. Walking haunched over they made their way into the mine entrance and cautiously moved into the mountain. They were looking for and searching for anything that may have been responsible for the killing of the guards.

Davos had rallied the remaining guards together at the camp. He was going to lead them through the Argian valley to continue his search for any ancient scrolls and to kill all that stood in his way. He started marching his part of the legion north. Moving steadily with the mountains to his west. They walked for several hours before they came across any sign of common folk. They had the first village insight. He moved the guards slowly around the outskirts of the village before ordering them to attack. The villagers were totally unaware of what was encroaching them from all sides. The guards rushed into the village setting fire to all the buildings and forcing the people out of them and out into the open. As they rushed from their homes they were brutally butchered as they ran for their lives. Men, women and children, all were slaughtered and all of their bodies were feeding the lands around them with blood.

Davos searched the village for anything that appeared to be of use to him. He found no magical items or scrolls that would help him. After they cleansed the village of all life they took what provisions they needed. They left the village behind them with all the buildings now nothing but charred wood and ash and the ground was strewn with bodies. As it did in the settlement camp all the trees and vegetation had started to rot and decay, turning from a bright flourishing green to nothing more than wilted weeds and black wooden stumps protruding from the ground. Davos and his army then continued their march northwards in search for the next village to be cleansed.

Back in the mines Jax and his guards had moved deep within them. They came across nothing so far, well nothing that he felt caused the death of his men. They did come across several more of the common folk that had escaped but they were easily disposed off. As they were brutally killed their screams echoed deep into mines allowing anyone in them to hear. Any other survivors that would of heard these screams would of known what was happening and what was searching for them. Jax and the guards knew that no matter how long it took them they had to keep searching the mines. Common folk were not what they were looking for. They kept moving forward down the one passage before they came to a cross section. He decided to divide his men so each passage could be searched at the same time. He sent four down the left passage and four down the right. The remaining four guards he took with himself down the centre. "Remember kill all that you come across." All three passageways were now being searched. There was no escape for anyone that was hiding down any of them. Jax could hear voices coming from ahead of him "faster, pick up the pace" they increased their pace to apprehend what was ahead of him. They got close enough to what was in-front of them and could see the movement of their shadows. They moved quickly around a corner expecting to find more common folk that were fleeing for their lives.

One of Jax's guards was the first to rush around the corner. The sound of a body hitting the ground could be heard by Jax and those that were with him, they then heard the sound of metal on metal. Before Jax and the others could move around the corner the helmet of the first guard rolled past their feet. Once they were around the corner they saw the guards body laying there before them, he had a large wound across his stomach, it was the same type of wound that Jax had found on the dead guards back at the settlement camp. The guard also had a second wound, only this was to the side of his head. It appeared to of been crushed. Judging from the damage caused to his skull this was caused by a heavy weapon, but the weapon used wasn't a bladed weapon, it was more like a large hammer that had hit him.

Return Of The Bloodstone

Jax and his men started to look around the area but they couldn't see anyone. They stripped the guard of anything that they thought would be useful to themselves. They left the body where it lay, bleeding out into the mine. Jax didn't notice but the ground in the mine wasn't absorbing the blood as it did in the settlement. "whatever is in here with us, we need to find it and kill it."

They continued to make their way though the passage. They still didn't see or hear anything ahead of them but yet they still continued to search deeper into the mine. They came to a small clearing which looked like a rest area. There was an old fire pit in the middle of it which didn't look like it had been used recently, next to that there were some mining tools leaning up against the wall. These were just tools, regular spikes, hammers and shovels but there was no sign of any weapons. Jax decided that they should rest, sit and wait while keeping perfectly still, hoping that they would hear something.

It didn't take long before they did hear something and it cut their rest short. They heard screams coming from the mine passage, but it wasn't the passage that they were following. "Quickly, follow me" Jax and his men gathered their weapons and started to head back the way that they had came. Soon they found themselves back at the passageway forks. "We go this way" he led them down the left side passage making sure that none of them rushed around any corners. They had moved a good distance down into the mine passage and ahead of them they could see the flickering of torch lights. Drawing out their swords they approached the area cautiously, not knowing what to expect. As they got closer to the light they saw what appeared to be bodies on the ground. They soon realised that they were bodies, there was four of them and all of them were his guards. All slaughtered as the others were. Whatever the weapons were that were being used to kill his guards they were large and dangerous.

The blades of these weapons were so large that they were able to slice straight through the guards armoured chest plates. After examining all the bodies more closely Jax managed to come to the conclusion that whatever it was they were looking for wanted them dead, they were being hunted.

He felt that they were being drawn into a trap. "We are not safe here, we are being thinned out, weakened we are being hunted." They turned around and left the bodies where they were before heading back towards the passage forks. They followed the right side passage hoping to get to the rest of his guards before they too fell victim to whatever it was in the mines. They moved at a fast steady pace doing their best to gain on the others.

They didn't come to any clearing as they did with the other passages, It was perfectly straight, there appeared to be no bends or corners to this passage, it just kept going straight. It didn't take them long and they soon saw as they did before, the flickering of firelight from oil burning torches. "You up there stop, it is I Jax" The movement of the torches in-front of them didn't appear to slow down. They just kept moving forward. They weren't going any slower or any faster "I command you to stop" It wasn't working, they weren't slowing down, they just kept walking. "faster follow me" Jax and the others started to move allot faster and they soon found themselves behind the others.

Jax shouted out to his men once more and as he did this the guards in-front of him stopped walking. He approached them and grabbed the last one in the line and turned him around. As the guard around he saw why they weren't able to answer, their mouths were gagged and their hands were bound to the torches. They were stripped of their weapons and had no means of defending themselves, they were bait, they were being used to lure Jax and the remaining guards to them. Jax had his guards quickly cut the binds and removed the gags. "Who did this to you?" One of the guards replied "I don't know, they came at us from all directions, before we realised what was happening we were knocked unconscious." "Quickly, we must keep walking" Once they were all untied from the binds and had the gags removed they all made their way down the passage as quietly as they could. They were being extra vigilant not to let their presence be known to whatever it was that was dwelling in the mines. They knew that whatever it was, it wasn't afraid of them and it was quite capable of defending itself.

Meanwhile Davos had marched his legion through many lands of the Argian valley. Distant fires could be seen from where they had been, bringing death and destruction to all they had encountered, slaughtering hundreds of common folk and destroying village after village, looking for the ancient scrolls that Blaine so desperately required.

The west side of the Argian valley bordering the

mountains had now become nothing more than a giant graveyard. The land had completely changed, it's appearance was now a dark and eerie one. The land had become lifeless, the shadows cast by the mountains upon these lands made the appearance of it all look even bleaker. The light shining down from the sun above was being shunned by the land, it was as if it had no place here, shining past the lands completely. The west side of the world had now changed. It had changed to a dark lifeless wasteland, it had changed to what Blaine is seeking for the whole world. Davos decided to rest his legion at the mountain's basin on the far side of the Argian Valley. They set up camp knowing that at some point Jax would return to them with his part of the legion.

Jax and his guards continued to walk through the mines. They didn't come across anything that attempted to cause him or his guards any harm. They were too deep into the mines to turn around and return the way that they entered. Continuing to be as quiet as they could they kept moving steadily forward, trying to find an exit from what appeared to be a stone tomb. They suddenly heard the sound of deep voices coming from further ahead of them. "Relinquish the torches" The guards did as they were ordered and put out their torches, they then continued to walk through the mines. They were now walking in darkness, unable to clearly see, not knowing what it was further ahead of them in the mines. As they got closer to the voices they then saw a light coming from a clearing ahead of them.

They slowly approached the light and it was only then that they were able to see what it was they had to confront, they were dwarves, the mountain was inhabited by dwarves. This explained the deep battle wounds that were inflicted upon his men, along with the heavy foot prints that they had found in the soil. "We need to get out of these mines and report these findings to Davos." They sat in the dark and waited for a while hoping that the dwarves would move on.

It didn't take long and several of the dwarves soon disappeared down one of the passages. This was the opportunity that Jax was waiting for. Leaning against one of the walls he could see his guards weapons. This confirmed to him that these were the ones responsible for disarming his guards and killing the others.

The mines were much higher here and Jax was able to stand tall, he walked into the clearing where the last two dwarves were stood. He didn't move in quietly, he was quite the opposite, he let his presence be known to them. "Taunt us, kill us, take what you can, I am here ready for you." The dwarves turned around to see who it was that was talking to them. They had killed some of the guards earlier but weren't expecting one to be quite as large as Jax. They got to their feet and ran towards their weapons. The first dwarf wasn't even able to make it several steps before Jax swung his sword fast and viscously slicing the dwarf across his waist. His blade was so sharp that it cleanly sliced straight through him. The dwarf's torso was completely separated as it hit the ground, his guts and blood were flowing heavily onto the stone floor of the mine. The second dwarf attempted to run down the same passage that his comrades had went down. Jax saw that he was attempting to escape and drew out a dagger, with one fast accurate throw his dagger was spinning through the air and sunk deep into the neck of his fleeing foe. "Bring me their heads." One of the guards walked up to the bodies of dwarves and decapitated them both.

"Now we leave these mines." The second passage from the clearing appeared to show a light at the end of it. It was too bright to be that of a torch so they assumed it was another entrance to the mines, this was their way out. The guards took back their weapons and they then all walked down the passage towards the light. Once they approached the end of the passage they realised that they were right, it was another entrance to the mines. It was far from the point at which they entered them, when they walked out into the open air they found themselves stood on the side of the mountain. Looking down into the valley they saw a dark land before them with fires burning in the distance. The fires that they were looking upon were giving off a thick black smoke. Jax and his guards made their way towards the closest fire. They knew that the fires they were heading towards were caused by the rest of the legion.

They found what appeared to be a well used path leading away from the mountain and down into the valley. After following this path they soon found themselves in familiar company. They had found their way to where Davos had set up camp. As they entered the camp they were greeted with large cheers from the guards that were there. Davos saw them approaching and walked towards Jax, "Well, are the mines cleansed?" "No my lord, but we have found what lurks within them." Jax walked towards Davos stopping directly in-front of him and dropped the heads from the two slaughtered dwarves at his feet.

Chapter 12

Blaine had spent many hours studying the book. Reading all he could from the blood soaked pages to obtain the knowledge that was hidden. He now had more understanding of what he needed in order to change this world. He knew that by bringing death and destruction to the world that it would naturally change to his desires. He didn't want to leave the now dark deserted city knowing that the one-thing he required was making its way to him and that it would soon be here.

Although he kept trying to draw evil and darkness from the vortex it wasn't being as successful as he had hoped. Delia's intervention had caused a disturbance in the magic that was cast upon it and reduced the darkness that was being drawn into the world. With his loyal demon hounds at his side he felt secure and safe. While In the city he also had with him the unholy army of shadow demons and night demons alike, but he knew that they couldn't stay here for long. He needed something more, he needed the return of the dark gemstones. The Bloodstone was one of the first that he required. He now had more understanding of the Bloodstone and how it works but what he truly required was a Night stone. The Night stone would give its holder the ability to change day to night and to call forth any demon or dark creature. He wanted a dark horde and he wanted to blacken out the sun. Making the day as night, a constant darkness across all the lands. Without the ancient scrolls he wouldn't know where to find the Night stone of which he so desperately wanted. One thousand year's earlier when Blaine's soul was imprisoned in the pearl the magical gemstones that couldn't be destroyed were scattered amongst the world. Scattered in the hope that no one would ever find them. If found then the evil powers that were bestowed upon them would no doubt return evil masters and darkness to all.

Blaine called forth his warlocks and witches before him, as they arrived he waited a short while before speaking to them, "Has no-one found any scrolls?" He failed to get a response "WELL" with all of them in fear of reporting failure none of them dare speak up. After a few moments of them all being stood in silence, one of the witches decided to speak, "No Master Blaine, we've searched many villages looking for any signs of the ancient scrolls but we haven't found anything. We've taken many lives of those refusing to aid us but there appears to be nothing to find." With the witch saying this Blaine stood to his feet, muttered and incantation and then before everyone she suddenly burst into flames. She was screaming in agony as the flames were burning the flesh from her bones. Her body dropped to the stone cold floor and nothing remained apart from her skeletal corpse and the stench of burnt flesh in the air.

This started to arouse the demon hounds that were stood amongst them, they started to growl deeply and pace the floor in circles. The warlocks and witches all looked scared not knowing what action Blaine was going to take next. Blaine opened his hands and pointed his palms to the floor, as he did this the demon hounds stopped growling and ceased pacing. Blaine looked at his followers and gave them a demand "go find me these scrolls, kill all who you must to get them, but I need these scrolls."

One by one his loyal followers left the temple but none of them used the door. They either disappeared into thin air or created a portal and stepped into it. After they left the temple hall Blaine was clearly enraged with the fact that none of them had found what he was looking for. He decided to look through the book of magic once more. He felt that he had missed something, he either wasn't reading it correctly or something was missing. Staring at the cover for several minutes longer he started to notice that the covering had images carved into it. Images of what appeared to look like gemstones. He thought nothing about it at first and then continued to read through the book.

As he was flipping through the pages he noticed that there was something different on several of them. At different sections of the book certain pages had darker lettering. They weren't set letters or at any set point but they were randomised throughout the whole book. He thought that this was strange so he started to study them more closely. He couldn't quite make out what they were or what they meant, that's if they actually meant anything at all.

He decided that if he couldn't physically see what they meant then maybe magic would reveal any hidden message. He went back to the first page that had these differences, he placed his hand over the page and closed his eyes before speaking, "Show me what is hidden, show me where to go," he moved his hand away from the page and as he opened his eyes it was there for him to see. All the darkened letters were now shining a bright yellow, with each letter joining to another. The section in the middle of all the glowing letter's showed him an image, it had the appearance of a map. He knew that the gemstones had been hidden away in the world and now he had an idea as to where. All he had to do now was to work out which gemstone was at each map section. After realising that he had all the answers in-front of him, he released a deep laughter that echoed throughout the temple hall.

Blaine had the first map piece directly in-front of him and was studying it closely. He had to work out where in the world this image being shown to him was. As for what was hidden there. He could only go on the assumption that the possible hidden gemstone was in relation to the magical spells on that page.

He started to do the same to each page that contained the highlighted lettering. He soon had multiple pages all showing what looked like different map sections. None of them were actually highlighting a set area of the world. He started to doubt that the pages were nothing and in frustration he started to tear them from the book. He ripped page after page from the book and as soon as he had finished tearing them all out he threw them across the floor. He sat back in his throne and put his head into his hands. He wanted more power and he knew that he needed the gemstones to obtain it. He was wondering what else it was that he had to do. He had sent out his legion to cause death and destruction across the lands, his warlocks and witches were searching for any know elders to obtain what information they could and yet he was still no closer to obtaining any stones with power.

He threw the book to the temple hall floor in disappointment. As he did this he started to feel a breeze blowing through the temple hall, "who's there, show yourself now." No one appeared before him, he could still feel the breeze blowing through the hall and it started to get stronger. The pages that were ripped from the book started to move across the floor. As the breeze got stronger the pages started to spin, as if they were in a whirlwind. Page after page they were adding themselves to the whirlwind that had magically appeared. It wasn't long before all the pages were spinning together and the light was getting brighter and brighter. Suddenly the wind had stopped. The paper that was trapped in the winds fell to the floor. Blaine looked on still waiting for someone to appear but no one did.

He looked to the floor where the paper had fell and he noticed that there was now only one piece. All the separate pages had bound together and formed one. He walked over to the paper and picked it up, he now had in his hand what appeared to be a parchment. Blaine started to look at it more closely and It was only at this moment he realised what had been formed, it was a map. A map of the world, but not as all currently know it, It was a map of the old world, a map when the world was in dark times. The places currently known to all were named differently and there were additional areas that weren't on any current maps. These areas were currently concealed by ancient magic and were hidden from sight to all.

This is where the gemstones would have been hidden and Blaine knew it. He now had the opportunity to obtain the power he sought. He again called forth all of his loyal followers, only this time he also called forth Davos. It didn't take them long before they all reappeared and were stood before him awaiting their master's commands. "I have now obtained the locations of what we seek. These locations have been hidden away for over a thousand years. You will claim them back in my name. Study this map and return to me what is mine." He lay the map down on a large iron table and the map of the old world was there for them all to see.

One at a time they approached the table and studied the map the best they could. The current world places were still there but they were all named differently. The northern seas were called the sea of souls, the eastern seas were named the blood rune waters. Strangely enough these two areas each had a magical gemstone found in them. The Pearl of souls was found in the sea of souls, and the Bloodstone was in the blood rune waters. Each section of the map appeared to be named after a different gemstone.

There were some sections on the old world map that none of the warlock's and witches had any knowledge about. Davos walked to the Iron table and looked over the map locating the wolf mountains. He saw what name they had in the old world and then he had to speak to his master." Master Blaine, we have cleansed the west side of the Argian valley, spilling enough blood that the soils have turned black and all life is wilting away. This area is ready for your demonic horde, the sun is now shunning this land." "Good Davos, you have done well." "However master, the mountains are inhabited. Jax lost several of his guards while cleansing out the common folk. He returned from the mines with two heads of his foes." "And what of it Davos, he has carried out your orders." "They were heads of dwarves master, the mountains are inhabited by dwarves and looking at the old world map it appears that they may never have left them." "What do you mean?" "The mountains were previously known as the Wardrun Mines. I have read about these before master. They were occupied by the mightiest of all the dwarves and they still occupy them." Blaine didn't want to hear any excuses, He looked at Davos and shouted "DON'T GIVE ME EXCUSES, YOU WILL CLEAR THEM OUT." All could see the fear in Davos's eyes as their master was clearly enraged. "Yes master."

So Davos was given his order's to clear out the mountain mines. He knew that Jax had lost several guards in the mountains and that taking control of them wasn't going to be easy. "Master, I will need several of the demon horde to take them faster. They can move through the darkness without being noticed." Blaine started to speak in the ancient language and then growling and snarling could be heard coming from the dark corners of the hall. Many night demons and shadow demons emerged from the darkness. Davos was again ordered to go and clear out the mountain mines. "Do not fail me Davos," Knowing that he had enraged his master, he left the temple hall as swiftly as he could taking with him several of the demons.

Blaine started to look over the map and he then realised

which areas that he needed to take control of first. The sea of souls was where the pearl was found and he knew that the blood rune waters was where the Bloodstone was being recovered.

He started to look over other areas of the map, trying to link the named lands to any lost gemstones of power. He wasn't sure where to start the search. He was hoping that Davos would clear the mines quickly so he could move his whole demonic horde there with no fear of sunlight destroying them.

He pointed to one area on the map and ordered the others to take control of the whole area. The area that he pointed to was the Argian Valley. On the old world map it was named Land of the dragon. He was hoping that in this area he would find what he wanted the most, the eye of the dragon, this is a magical ruby which looks just like a dragon's eye, it was was said to of had great powers. He knew that if this gemstone could be found then nothing was going to stop him from claiming the world. They all left the hall and started to appear in the valley. They weren't on their own though, Blaine was with them. He wanted to be part of the cleansing, he wanted to be part of the devastation caused.

They appeared in the central part of the Argian Valley and it didn't take them long to come across their first village. They found very little resistance here and were easily able to over power the common folk. They didn't have swords or daggers as the guards did but they were killing common folk using magic. Some were killed by magically having their skulls crushed, others were instantly combusting into flames and what appeared to be the worst method of brutality was that many of them had their hearts ripped from their chests. The buildings were all set fire to and anyone hiding within them soon came running out, either in fear or whilst burning in flames. The Argian's had no chance of survival against the evil powers that were now here in their part of the world.

Blaine ordered his warlocks and witches to the next village. They moved across the lands quickly as smoke in the air and not in physical form. Moving further north, they soon came across the next village. They switched from their mystical form to physical form and started to walk into the village. As they entered the village they realised that there was no-one there. No men, no women and no children, all the people were gone. Suddenly they could hear a whistling sound cutting through the air above them. As they turned to see what it was several of the warlocks and witches were impaled by a downpour of arrows. They were being attacked, they had found the village which had formed an army. Blaine and several of his warlocks quickly moved back to their mist form and reappeared on a different side of the village.

As they did this they again heard the same sound of arrows cutting through the air. Several of them were quick to move from the area while others were too slow and were killed as a volley of arrows rained down upon them. Blaine realised what was happening, he quickly ordered them to stay in their mist form and move out of the village. They all reappeared on the east side of the village and were stood looking in. Blaine soon arrived amongst them and told them to return to the temple hall and wait for his arrival.

He waited a while and was stood still in the darkness, just watching the village. He soon heard the sound of cheering coming from villagers and he then saw them returning to the village centre. He let as many of them enter the village as possible and once the village was populated again he pulled his hood up over his head and slowly walked towards them.

Several of the villagers noticed him approaching and ran to get the fighter's and the elders. They rushed to the side of the village that Blaine was entering from and they then formed a defensive line. Blaine walked to within a few steps from them before starting to speak. "Who here is an elder?" one of the fighter's shouted out "They don't want to speak with you." Blaine now knew that there wasn't one elder here but several. He asked again "Who here is an elder?" This time an old man walked forward towards Blaine "what do you want?" Blaine lifted his head and removed his hood. Voices could be heard from the crowd, "That's Colias" "No it's not." "I think it is." The elder then spoke "Why have you come to our lands" why have you come here to kill" why have you returned to our world?" Blaine gave the old man a long dark stare "I am here for what is mine" "Nothing here is yours." "This world was mine and this world will be mine again." he turned from the old man and started to walk away. The crowd of villagers were jeering him as he was walking away and then suddenly loud screams could be heard.

The villagers that were stood behind Blaine were now running around in a panic, running for their lives. Night demons had appeared amongst the crowd and were savaging as many of the villagers as they could. They tried their hardest to fight back against them but it was useless, they were too difficult to see, they were too fast and they were too brutal. During the savage attack the demons had managed to rip apart and slaughter many villagers. The killings continued until Blaine had disappeared completely from the area and they then disappeared with him.

Several elders were stood over the bodies of their kin and witnessed the blood from the slaughtered being absorbed by the land. One of them looked up from what he was witnessing and spoke to the others "This will soon be his world, the lands are opening up to his will. We must prepare." They left the area and informed all in the village that they must seek a sanctuary where they can be more secure. "You must all carry what you can and head west. Go to the wolf mountains, enter the mines and seek out the Wardrun king." Not many knew what the Wardrun was, the elders knew the true name of the mountains as it had been passed on to them through generations of teaching. In a mass panic the village started to empty with the common folk carrying all that they could.

Blaine was back in the temple hall and was assessing how many of his warlocks and witches he had lost. He now only had a few left with him that had strong magical abilities. Not only did he need to protect them he needed to teach them, he needed them to grow in power and strength. He needed not just demons and fighters in his legion but he needed strong merciless magicians.

While he was with them he asked them all a question, "Whom of you have undertaken the trials?" they all looked at Blaine not knowing how to respond or if they even should. "well, has no-one here undertaken the sacred trials?" One of the witches walked forward and spoke "I have undertaken the trials master." "What did you defeat?" "I didn't defeat anything master, I was to show all the magic that I could perform against another and if strong enough I was informed of being successful." "Have any of you had to defeat a magical beast in your trials?" None of them responded with a yes. The old ways of undertaking the trials wasn't taught to them. In time the method of undertaking the trials had became obscure and obsolete, only a few carried on the practice such as Gideon, Sloan and possibly others yet to be known.

Blaine informed them all to leave his sight and to prepare themselves for the sacred trials. He was either going to have stronger magicians beside him or none at all.

Chapter 13

We had finally made it out of the cavern passageways and we were surprised to see where we were. The first thing we did was start to look around the arena and what we were looking upon had totally shocked us. There was a large hole in the centre of the fighting pit with black smoke slowly seeping from it and the sunlight that was shining into the arena was quickly dispersing it.

We could hear movement around us but we weren't able to see anything. "Sloan, what do we do with the Bloodstone," "I'm not too sure Mickel, but we need to get closer to that vortex to see what exactly it is." There were several city guards on patrol along the arena walls but there were none down in the fighting pit where we were. Athian started to walk around the arenas edge, trying several of the gates to see if any of them would open. "Athian, stay close to us, don't wander off." "It's okay Sloan, I'm just checking to see if we have a way out." Krissy decided to stay with Athian to ensure that he kept insight and didn't bring any unwanted attention to us.

Sloan pulled his hood up over his head and started to

walk towards the vortex. "Mickel you come with me." They slowly made their way to the middle of the arena. Although there were city guards in the arena none of them shouted at them or moved towards them in an attempt to stop them.

They got close enough to the edge of the vortex that they were able to peer down into the large hole that was there. "He's created a gateway, this is where the darkness is coming from." What do you mean?" "Down in there is a different realm, he's merging that realm with our world." We didn't realise it but while at the vortex the Bloodstone had started to glow brighter. It was drawing the black smoke from the vortex into it.

Krissy and Athian were looking on the edge of the fighting pit and they had noticed this and ran across to them "What are you doing?" At the time neither Sloan or myself knew what they were talking about." "we're just looking into the vortex." "No, look at Sloan, look at the Bloodstone." I moved my attention away from the vortex and that's when I noticed that Sloan's holding pouch was glowing a bright red. I noticed that the black smoke was being absorbed into it. "Sloan, the Bloodstone, look at it." Sloan looked to his pouch and saw what was happening. He removed the Bloodstone from the animal hide that it was wrapped in. He could see how brightly the stone was shining and he noticed that the black smoke was being absorbed into it. With the Bloodstone in his hand he could clearly see what was happening. "It's magic was working, it was absorbing evil and darkness." Athian was just stood staring at it in amazement. "It looks like it's breathing." I know it sounded crazy hearing Athian say this but he was right. Again the Bloodstone appeared to be pulsating like it was alive. It had the same action as lungs do when we breathe, expanding a little with every absorption of black smoke.

Only Sloan clearly understood what was happening. "We need to leave this area now." Before the guards got too suspicious we quickly left the arena centre. Athian had managed to find several open gates and we decided to seek refuge in one of them. We made our way beneath the arena stands and found ourselves in one of the holding chambers. These felt very familiar as we've been in them before. Only this time they weren't full of fighters but they were full of corpses and body parts. "It stinks in here, we can't stay here." Athian was right the smell was a horrid putrid stench that was making us all feel sick. The holding chambers were in complete darkness, they had now become the safe haven for the demons that had been emerging from the vortex.

We started to move through the cells hoping that we could find a more suitable place to hide. Sloan directed us into one cell and cast an incantation across the cell's gate. "we will be safe here, I have hidden this cell from the sight of other's." Although it wasn't where we wanted to be, it did smell better than the others. "What do we do now Sloan." "now we must make a decision." "What decision?" "Yeah Sloan, what must we decide." It's not a decision for all of us to make, I am only the holder. Mickel must make the decision." None of us were fully sure why Sloan said that we all couldn't make the decision. We knew what the elder had told him but we still didn't quite know the decision that had to be made, the choice that Mickel had to make.

Return Of The Bloodstone

We waited in the cell for a while thinking about what we were going to do next. We could hear movement from the corridor outside of the cell and then we could hear heavy breathing, it was the sound of something big sniffing the air. It got closer to our cell and then we could see it. It was a large demon, It's eyes were blacked out and it had large red blood veins across its body and head. It stopped right in-front of our cell sniffing the air deeply. It was looking for us, it must of picked up our scent and was tracking us. It didn't make an attempt to enter the cell so Sloan's spell was clearly working, we were hidden from it. "I will show you this now Mickel and you will understand what decision it is that you have to make." Sloan removed the Bloodstone and we all saw that it was again pulsating and glowing bright. He walked closer towards the cell gate next to where the demon was stood on the other side.

We all stood and looked on in fear, worried that the demon would sense Sloan's presence and would enter the cell to attack us. As Sloan got closer to the beast we saw that the Bloodstone was pulsating faster. The demon that was stood opposite Sloan started to stare deep into the cell that we now felt trapped in. We started to notice a difference in the demon, it was swaying side to side, moving slowly and it's legs had started to give way. It slumped to the ground of the corridor and we could hear it's breathing getting slower and slower. "What's happening to it Sloan." asked Athian. "The evil that is in this demon is being drawn out of it. It is being drawn into the Bloodstone." "But the demon looks like it is dying." It is Krissy, there's nothing else within it to keep it alive. Mickel do you understand what this means?" "I think I do Sloan. We could use it to draw Blaine out of my father's body." "Yes Mickel, or we could use it to close the vortex and stop these beasts from entering our world. The decision is yours."

After looking at the corpse of the demon we all moved back into the cell keeping as quiet as we could and remaining hidden from any-more demons that may be lurking in the corridors. Knowing now that there was a way to bring Colias back, Mickel seemed to distance himself from the others, he had a big decision to make. It was now clear what the elder had told Sloan. Mickel could either decide to save his father and let the world face the evil that will soon flood it or he could prevent more evil from entering our world and live with the fact that his father is gone.

Sloan started to wrap the Bloodstone back into it's parchment and was just about to put it back into his holding pouch. Athian suddenly spoke. "Sloan why is the Bloodstone looking darker." We all looked at it and noticed that the bright red patches had now started to appear darker. It was still red but with black patches appearing upon it again. "It is absorbing darkness Athian, once it has absorbed all the darkness it can it will no longer be able to draw evil from anything else. This is something you need to understand Mickel. You have one opportunity to decide how you want me to use the Bloodstone, after this we may never find another, so we may never be able to attempt the same thing again." "I understand Sloan."

Mickel was in deep thought, knowing that one decision may be right for himself and his friends but that it could be the wrong decision for the rest of the world. He also knew that if he made the decision for the world then he would possibly hate himself for the rest of his life. It was a difficult situation that he had found himself in, he knew that he had to make up his mind and that he had to do it quickly.

They were sat silently waiting in the cell when they could hear noises coming from the arena. "What's that." Asked Athian. "I'm not too sure." replied Sloan. Although the one decision was Mickel's to make, they all decided together that they would leave the cell to see where the noises were coming from. They walked down the corridor slowly and soon found themselves at the gate peering into the arena. They couldn't see anyone in the arena basin but they could hear voices coming from the arena stands. They looked around and that's when they saw him. Blaine was stood on the master's platform with several warlocks and witches. "So who's to be first." no one replied to what Blaine had asked. He grabbed one of the warlocks around the throat, lifted him high into the air and threw him down into the arena. Blaine appeared to be a lot more stronger now than what he was before.

The warlock was stood in the arena on his own. Blaine spoke and incantation and thrust his hands down towards the arena. It appeared to look like red lightning that came from his hands and as it struck the ground directly in-front of the warlock it created a large red dust cloud. The dust cloud was moving in the air, it was forming together and had started to take shape. As the shape was forming we all heard what sounded like a loud hissing sound, we then noticed what it was. The cloud had completely disappeared and formed into a giant snake. It wasn't a normal looking snake, it had two heads and appeared to have no tail. "what the hell is that." "It is an Amphisbaena

Snake Athian." "A what? I've never heard of such a thing." "I've only ever read about them, It's a snake with two heads and no tail, each head carries a deadly venom which it can induce by biting or spitting. They are very difficult to fight against."

Once the giant Amphisbaena snake was fully formed it didn't hesitate to strike towards the warlock. The warlock managed to evade it's strikes several times before eventually casting some spells of his own against it.

The snake was hit several times but the spells didn't appear to have much of an effect against it. As one head launched an attack and was moving backwards in retreat the second head was ready to strike. This made it very difficult for the warlock to fight against. He had to be quick with his mind and not just rely on physical speed. Strike after strike the snake was trying to bite the warlock or spit it's venom on him. The warlock had called forth a shielding spell which was helping him block what was coming towards him, he didn't know how to stop this beast from constantly attacking him.

He launched several fire spells towards this beast, striking it several times but they appeared to have very little effect. He had to do something, Blaine was watching on from above and he knew that if he didn't show strength then there would be no place in Blaine's world for him. He kept attacking the one head, but as nothing was happening he tried a spell against the left sided head. He launched a fireball fast and directly at it, it struck the Amphisbaena and then suddenly it backed away screaming in pain. That was it, he had found a weakness, although one head was able to resist magic the other one wasn't. The warlock again launched the same attack against it aiming for the same head and again the beast was in retreat and pain, screaming louder and hissing with more aggressive intent.

The warlock was preparing one large spell which he was hoping would win him this battle and a place by his master's side. As he was preparing the incantation the giant beast started to move side to side, wrapping itself around itself. The warlock didn't know what it was doing, he had now lost focus and he didn't know which head was the one that magic was able to inflict pain upon.

He called forth a lightning spell and launched it forward towards the now entangled heads, he was hoping that he was going to hit the right one. With the lightning strike heading directly towards the Amphisbaena it quickly started to untwist itself, the lighting hit the snake directly in one head however the other launched forward and managed to strike the warlock. The warlock was instantly paralysed, completely unable to move. As the one head moved backwards the second one then struck and bit the warlock in half. Blaine was watching on from his platform "Weak and pathetic, have any of you learned anything?" He grabbed a different warlock and as with the first he also threw this one down into the arena.

We kept quiet watching, not knowing exactly what was happening. I decided to ask if Sloan knew "Sloan what's happening?" "It's the sacred trials Mickel, he is putting his warlocks and witches through the sacred trials. If he succeeds then the dark magic in this world will only be stronger." As we watched on we saw that the second warlock was doing the same as the first. He called forth a shielding spell to protect himself from the incoming strikes and venom. He seemed a lot more patient than what the first warlock was. He must of watched and learnt from the others mistakes. He didn't launch any fire or lightning attacks against the snake instead he tried something completely different. He launched what looked like a wall of water. The giant Amphisbaena was moving backwards from this wall of water, showing fear of it. The water was moving, encroaching closer to it's target and once close enough it started to twirl around the giant beast. It formed a full circle which left the giant snake in what appeared to be a giant water orb. It was unable to launch any strikes against the warlock, the warlock was concentrating hard to maintain his spell. With the giant Amphisbaena being engulfed by water it appeared to be drowning. We could hear the hissing and screaming coming from it. Eventually we saw that it had stopped moving completely. As the warlock lowered his arms and stopped the spell the water orb lost all of it's shape. A wall of water came splashing down into the arena, along with it, one dead two headed reptile. A voice was then heard from the watching master "Well done, you have earned your place by my side." The warlock disappeared from the arena and reappeared standing next to Blaine. "What is your name?" The warlock looked at his master and replied, "I am Marcus of the Southern Ice Fields." The Southern Ice fields are an area below the Mining Islands. Not many dare venture that far south due to the extreme cold. Those that do reside there are able to grow in strength and power as they are isolated from all others.

The trials then continued and other warlocks and witches were successfully defeating the beasts that Blaine had conjured up for them to battle. "We can't let this continue Sloan." "You're right Krissy, we must do something to stop these trials." Blaine now had four strong mages that had successfully defeated their trial, it was more than double this number that had failed, the trials were a success.

The last one was now in the arena and was about to undertake their trial when Davos suddenly appeared. "Master we are about to enter and take the Wardrun mines but I have come to inform you that my scouts have reported thousands of common folk moving through the Argian valley towards the mountains." Blaine had realised that with his actions at the village the common folk were moving on to a safe place. They were seeking sanctuary in the mines. "Just as I expected, confront them and kill them all before they reach the mountains. The land there must be turned to blackness."

Blaine knew that the lands in the Argian valley were accepting darkness and the darkness will grow from spilt blood. He anticipated that with his actions in the village they would flee the area, gathering more people with them as they crossed the lands. This meant more innocent to die, more blood for the lands and a larger area of darkness. "These here have passed their trials. Take them with you and add them to the legion that you currently control." Davos, Marcus and the other mages left the arena and went to the west side of the Argian valley. They gathered together the legion of city guards and started to march eastwards towards the oncoming common folk.

With everything that was happening in the arena none of them had noticed that the vortex was now becoming more active. With the dark powers in the world now growing stronger, the darkness from within the vortex was being drawn into our world. "Sloan, look at the vortex." Sloan looked over to see that there was now more black smoke being pulled into our world. The black shroud above the city had once again started to form. Our world was not just drawing darkness from the other realm but it was also drawing in more dark creatures. "Mickel, we need to act now, the decision is yours." Mickel now had to make a decision that will benefit either himself or the world. "Sloan, I believe if we stop Blaine then we can stop all of this from happening and maybe, just maybe I will also have my father back." "I can't decide for you Mickel, you must make the decision."

Mickel knew that the reason for the world's change into darkness was because of him. He tried to save his father once but failed. He now has a second opportunity to save him and understood that if he failed again then the world would truly suffer. "Sloan, I have decided. Take the Bloodstone to the vortex. Stop this evil from entering our world." Sloan acknowledged what Mickel was asking, "Athian you must come with me and when I speak you must repeat exactly what I say." Sloan and Athian made their way across to the vortex.

As they got closer to the vortex Sloan could feel the Bloodstone getting heavier. Krissy and Mickel walked out into the arena and called out Blaine's name. "Blaine, we are here for you." Blaine stood up on this platform and looked down to see who it was that was calling out his name. As he looked down into the arena his eyes started to glow a bright red. He mystically moved his way through the air and stood before them, "Well Mickel, we meet again. Young lady, you still look a pretty little thing, even with the scar." Krissy put her hand to her head and covered the wound that Blaine had inflicted upon her a year earlier.

Mickel was trying to distract Blaine the best he could. "You tricked me, where's my father?" With a wicked grin across his face and a deep laugh, Blaine just looked at Mickel like he was a fool. "Your father was weak, he has no place here in this world. He offered himself unto me willingly." "You lie, what have you done with him?" Blaine didn't show any emotion on his face at all, he just looked at Mickel and asked "would you like to see him again?" "You know I would." Blaine's face started to change, his eyes went from red to blue, the black veins disappeared and the dark skin complexion got lighter. Mickel looked on in disbelief "Father" he couldn't believe what he was seeing, he was looking again at his fathers face. A tear wept from his eye and started to roll down his cheek.

As he was in this state of mind Blaine quickly transformed his image back to that of his own, using a magic spell he threw Mickel across the grounds of the arena. Krissy instantly drew out her daggers and with her arms stretched out she quickly spun herself around. Her blades sliced straight across Blaine's arm and chest, cutting him deep. Blood started to flow from the wounds she had inflicted, it wasn't normal blood, it was as black as the night and as thick as tar. Blaine didn't appear to let it effect him. He forced Krissy across the arena and pulled Mickel towards him. He held Mickel high in the air "do you really think you can stop me?" He then dropped Mickel to the ground and looked down at him with nothing but hate and anger in his eyes. Suddenly Blaine put his hands to his head as if he was in agonising pain.

Sloan and Athian had left the area of the vortex and Sloan was pressing the Bloodstone hard against Blaine's head. The Bloodstone was starting to turn black, it was draining the evil that was in Colias's body. Blaine dropped to his knees as he was losing all thought and consciousness. "Mickel, quickly come here and talk to your father." The image of Colias had once again returned to his face. The Bloodstone was getting darker and darker "father, is that you?" The image of Colias was now clear for all to see. "Yes Mickel, It's me." Athian came running across to speak to him also. "Colias sir, you wouldn't believe what's happened to me." "not now Athian we don't have time. "Mickel, it is I your father, you need to listen to me very carefully. You can't let Blaine take control of this world, close the vortex. Stop the evil that is coming into our world." "But father, how do I close the vortex?" Sloan will know how, he's doing it now to Blaine. The Bloodstone draws in evil from people or objects." "But what will happen to you." "I have been gone a long time now son, I could never return. You can stop what Blaine has started." Just as Mickel was about to ask his father another question he saw the image of Blaine returning and his fathers fading. Blaine was resisting the power of the Bloodstone, he was fighting it's will to draw him out and was forcing the soul of Colias back deep inside himself."

Now is the moment that Mickel had to make his decision. He paused for a moment and then decided what had to be done. "Sloan, go and close the vortex, now Sloan, go now." Sloan and Athian both ran back towards the vortex. Sloan had started to speak an incantation and Athian was repeating exactly what he heard but nothing appeared to be happening.

Not far from them Krissy and Mickel were both struggling to contain Blaine. He was nearly back to himself and they knew that they wouldn't be able to contain him for much longer. "Nothings happening Sloan" "keep repeating the spell Athian, don't stop." Sloan was holding the Bloodstone over the opening of the vortex while constantly speaking the incantation. They then suddenly noticed something was happening. There was a heavy pulsating coming from the Bloodstone. The black smoke from the vortex was being drawn into it. The black shroud overhead was forming into whirlwind, this was also being pulled down towards Sloan's hands. Demons could be seen moving out of the darkness and heading towards the vortex. They weren't being aggressive but they were being more submissive. As several of them got close enough to the vortex they could be seen to shrivel and wilt before dying and their bodies hitting the ground. The Bloodstone was working, it was drawing anything evil and dark into it.

Krissy and Mickel were physically trying to confront Blaine. They tried multiple attempts to attack him but they all failed. Blaine forced his arms out to his side and both Mickel and Krissy were thrown across the arena with ease, both of them hitting the walls hard and falling unconscious. He started to walk towards Sloan and Athian. As Sloan saw Blaine walking towards them he told Athian to close his eyes. Athian didn't question Sloan and closed his eyes as he was asked to do. Once Sloan could see that Athian's eyes were closed he dropped the Bloodstone into the vortex. It dropped down to ground level but didn't appear to sink completely into the vortex. The ground around the whole arena started to shake vigorously, the black cloud above us in the skies was now being pulled to the ground fast. Just as Blaine got to within a few steps of Sloan and Athian there was a blinding flash of light with an explosive force that accompanied it.

The bang was so strong that it shook the whole arena and most of the buildings in the city. Sloan and Athian were both sent flying through the air from the explosive force. Blaine was pushed so hard backwards that even he couldn't resist the power. Everyone in the Arena was now unconscious and totally unaware of what had just happened.

Chapter 14

Blaine was the first one to get back to his feet. He walked to where the vortex was and brushed the debris and dust cloud to one side. He looked around the arena and saw the aftermath of what had just happened. His four foes were laying either unconscious or dead around the arena. The arena structure showed severe damage and parts of it were starting to crumble. The black roots that had covered the arena had now wilted away once again revealing the stone structure and statues that laid beneath them.

The skies above were no longer filled with the evil black cloud and sunlight had once again started to shine into the city. Blaine tried to call forth his demon horde but none came to his side. He looked to the ground around him and he noticed that the vortex was gone. Whatever had happened with the Bloodstone it had managed to completely close the vortex. The magical powers drawing the evil in from another realm had been stopped. Mickel and the others had done it, they had managed to stop the vortex from changing the world.

Blaine looked to the ground hoping to see the Bloodstone but it wasn't there to be found. He did see something else though, he knelt down to one knee and picked it up the item that he found. An evil grimace then came over his face, he put what he had found into his robe pocket and stood back to his feet.

What Sloan and the others didn't know that there was too much evil and darkness for the Bloodstone to safely contain. No one knew that the Bloodstone drawing in so much power would cause the chaos and destruction that it did. Blaine now had in his possession something that he was hoping would give him more power to change the world. A power that even he himself didn't think he would be able to fully control. This was an item that he had to keep, the holder of this item would have the power to call forth anything dark and demonic, he would even have the power to turn day to night, the Bloodstone had fused itself with all the evil that it absorbed and a Night Stone was created.

With Blaine now having an item of such importance he decided to leave the city. He didn't even bother to check if his enemies were wounded or dead. He changed his form to the dark mist and disappeared into the air, abandoning the now sunlit crumbling city behind him. While holding his head in discomfort Mickel was the first to stir from his unconsciousness and managed to get to his feet. Not far from him he saw Krissy laying on the ground under a pile of rubble. He quickly rushed across to her and started to remove any stones and timber that he could. Once she was able to freely move he then moved across to where Athian and Sloan were. He saw that Sloan was sitting up and appeared to be okay so he focussed his attention on helping Athian. It took Athian a while to fully get his bearings back but he was okay. "What happened?"

Sloan started to explain what the Bloodstone had done. "The Bloodstone was drawing in darkness. It had absorbed so much darkness and evil that it wasn't able to contain it." "But where's the Bloodstone now." "I'm not sure Mickel, all I know is that the it's and so is the vortex." Until Sloan had said this the other's didn't even realise that the vortex had closed. They all looked to where the vortex was and none of them could see the Bloodstone, it wasn't anywhere to be found. However where the Bloodstone was dropped there was a small pit, it appeared to be made of black sand.

They were all now in the middle of the arena and were

tending to their wounds. Looking around the arena they could see that the black roots that had grown everywhere were gone. They now had the appearance of what looked like wilted dying Ivy plants. Although the stone structures of the arena were now again visible they no longer appeared to be safe. There were plenty of sections in the arena that had crumbled and many of the gate entrances were completely blocked.

Mickel was stood close to where the vortex was, he bent down to one knee and was looking at the thin black sand that was at his feet. "what are you looking at Mickel." I don't know Sloan, It looks like something was here, there's an indentation in this black sand. I think some-things been removed." "I'm sure it's nothing Mickel, it's probably just the remnant remains of where the Bloodstone landed."

They were all thinking that as the arena wasn't safe they needed to leave it. They found a safe exit point and made their way out of the arena. They started walking through the city and saw that many of the buildings were crumbled and destroyed. From the year of darkness in the city there were skeletal corpses scattered everywhere. As they walked through the streets they saw no common folk, no city guards and no demons. Even though no-one or anything demonic could be seen they still walked as carefully and as quietly as they could. "Where is everyone" "I don't know Athian, but let's still keep a watchful eye as we walk these streets."

Working our way through all the debris we soon found made it to the temple. The walls here were no longer covered in the giant black roots that we had used to gain entrance. It was as if all evil in the city had completely been drawn away. When we arrived at the temple we noticed that the entrance was clearly visible. The magical incantation that had kept it hidden from normal view had faded. We walked very cautiously through the entrance as we didn't know what may be lurking inside. When we entered we noticed that here too it was also empty, completely abandoned. There was an eerie silence about the place.

As we stood in the hall it was exactly as we remembered it, apart from the corpses and body parts that lay scattered across the floor that is. These were most likely to of been remains from people that fell victim to the demons.

We started to search the hall looking for anything that we could use, such as food, water or weapons. Suddenly Sloan told us all to be quiet "Shush, do you hear that?" We all stood completely still and started to listen intently for what it was that Sloan had heard. A few moments had passed and then we all heard it. We all heard a voice, It sounded like the voice was coming from beneath us. We paused a little while and then we all heard it again. It was definitely beneath us, it was coming from the dungeon, possibly the very same dungeon that Colias was held and tortured in.

We couldn't see anywhere that led down into the dungeon. We started to search the whole of the temple hall looking for any steps that led downwards. We all searched for several minutes before Krissy spoke out, "Mickel over here" In the back area of the temple hall hidden in darkness Krissy had found something that looked like steps leading down. There was a wall running parallel alongside another. It was a passage hidden in the darkness and in the passage there were steps that led us to what looked like the dungeon. It wasn't a very wide passage and there was barely enough room for one person to fit through it. We all entered the passage separately and followed the steps down. It was definitely the right area that we were looking for. The further down the steps they went the louder the murmuring voice became. they eventually came to the bottom of the steps and they could hear a voice coming from the far end of a long dark corridor.

Amongst us all Krissy was the most dangerous fighter so she decided that she would walk ahead of us. She walked slowly down the corridor and eventually reached the far cell. As she got to the cell she peered into it and inside she saw a man slumped in the corner "help me, please help me." Sloan was now stood right behind Krissy. He saw that the cell gate was locked and using his brute strength he was able to force the chains apart. He slowly opened the steel gate and entered the cell. He walked towards the man and as he reached him he put his hand on the man's shoulder. With the man feeling this he slowly turned his head and looked up. "help me."

The man was badly beaten and his hands were bound together with iron chains. The chains had magical glyph symbols upon them, he was imprisoned by magic to not be able to use magic. Sloan tried to break these chains as he did with chains on the gate. These chains weren't breaking, he was physically unable to break them. He then tried to use a magical incantation, he closed his eyes and placed his hands over the chains, he spoke a few words and then the chains suddenly broke into two.

The man was now able to freely use his hands. Although he had been tortured and was shaking from the from cold he was able to stand to his feet. In pain and discomfort he slowly turned around. He started to walk out of the darkness towards the lightly lit entrance. As he stood in the entrance of the cell he lifted his head and looked directly at those that were stood in front of him "Gideon, is that you? Is it really you?" Krissy could clearly see the face of the man who had brought her up, the one who had looked after her and taught her all that she knew "Yes Krissy, it's me" Gideon was alive.

We all left the creepy dungeon and made our way back up the steps into the hall. They sat Gideon down so he wasn't in too much discomfort. Krissy sat with him just holding his hands and crying. She couldn't believe that he was alive, in fact none of us could. For a whole year we all thought that Gideon was dead. Once she had cried all the tears of sorrow and joy away she started to tend to his wounds. He was so weak from being tortured and locked away that he wasn't able to heal himself. "Here let me help" Sloan knelt down next to them and started to heal some of the bad wounds that his old master had obtained. "Athian, bring me some water" Athian started to look around the hall for some much needed water. Earlier he thought that he had taken all the good water, but he managed to find some more. Although it didn't look the cleanest of water it was better than none.

Sloan used the same healing powers that his old master used on him and he managed to heal up some of Gideon's bad wounds. Gideon had eventually managed to refresh himself and was able to speak more clearly "what was that loud explosive bang, what has happened?" "It was a Bloodstone, we managed to close a vortex from a dark realm with it." We all took turns explaining to Gideon what we had been through. Finding the Bloodstone, fighting the sea dragon and making our way here into the city.

Before we managed to explain to him about the Bloodstone drawing in the evil and darkness from the city he somehow must of already known. "what did the Bloodstone absorb? What life force went into it?" "It absorbed many things, life force from demons, dark clouds, the vortex and even some of the evil from Blaine." "We think it absorbed too much negative energy and it destroyed itself." Gideon stood to his feet and using a spell he managed to clean himself up, his clothes had completely changed, his hair suddenly got shorter and his face appeared to change, it had slightly healed and he looked cleaner and younger than we remembered him looking. He then started to speak again, "where's the Night Stone?" "Where's the what" asked Athian. "The Night Stone, where is the Night tone?" "There was no Night Stone Gideon, we had a Bloodstone" None of us were completely sure why Gideon was showing so much concern over this Night Stone. All we knew was that we had a bloodstone and with it we had an opportunity to stop evil. Gideon listened to all that we had to say and he then started to explain to us the power of a Bloodstone. "The Bloodstone absorbs negative life force, purifying whatever it draws the evil out of. If it absorbs too much darkness for it to contain then it will implode, compressing all the darkness and evil together forming a Night Stone. In the hands of the wrong person a Night Stone is a very dangerous stone of power, not just to the holder but to the world. The holder of the it will have the ability to call forth all different types of dark beings. Most of these will be under his command to do any bidding that he wishes. Should the holder learn how to use the it correctly then they will have the power to black out the sun. With no natural light in the world all types of demons will be able to stalk the lands freely."

They all now partially understood what had happened. They realised that the Bloodstone had changed and that Blaine had taken the Night Stone that was created from it. The city had been purified of the evil and darkness that had been previously present. Blaine and the darkness that enshrouds him had completely left the city, but where Blaine had gone to, none of us knew. We had to locate him and the legion that he commands before it was too late. We all listened intently to what Gideon was telling us, none us truly knew how powerful the gemstones were. Athian and myself always thought that the stories told to us were exaggerated.

Although Gideon had been locked away in the dungeon cells for a year he told us that he had heard many discussions from the temple hall. Voices echoed clearly down into the dungeon cells. He told us that Blaine was brutal in his obsession of dominating the world. He said that he knew the legion was heading north and that the mountains were going to be the main area for him to start changing the world.

We all looked at each other showing grave concern. We had left many common folk at the base of the mountains and none of them were battle hardened fighters. "We have to get back to our settlement. We need to warn and help the people that we have left there."

Return Of The Bloodstone

Sloan was in complete agreement with Mickel, he also knew that the people left behind to guard the book of magic would be no match for the evil legion that was heading towards them. They had to get back to them quickly.

Athian and Krissy both knew if they were to go back to the settlement that they may not like what they would encounter there. "Why can't we stay here, evil is gone from here now, we are safe here." "Athian, these people are villagers just like you and I, you know they need our help?" Gideon raised his head and spoke sternly towards all of us "Athian is right, we need to stay safe and secure, we need an area for others to be safe in also. We need to stay here for now." "Master, the boys are both right, we need to help the common folk and have a safe place away from the evil." Krissy then sat down and didn't say another word. Gideon stood to his feet "we must remain here in the city, this will be our sanctuary. The city is cleansed of evil, this will be a safe haven for all." Gideon then left the temple and walked out into the city. They all followed him to see where he was going. He stood in-front of the temple and raised his hands high above his head before speaking an incantation, he told Sloan and Athian to join him. "Close you eyes and concentrate your thoughts on light and positive energy. They did exactly as Gideon had requested.

After a few minutes of standing still and concentrating, a light started to rise from all of their hands. It rose higher than the temple itself and started to spread outwards, spreading out past the city walls before suddenly dropping to the ground and in an instant the light faded. The walls on the edge of the city where the light reached had a shimmering effect to them. "What's just happened" asked an Elder. Sloan then explained to them what Gideon had done. "We've just put a warding shield around the city. The area inside the shimmering dome is now protected against evil, it will keep out any supernatural beings. It will not however keep out the city guards. We need to go now and save your people, we will return here with them. We must prepare for what future this world will have."

We all started to gear ourselves up for yet another quest. It appears that we never get time to completely relax any more. There's always something that we need to do. As we were preparing our weapons and packs we all heard Athian scream. We rushed over to where he was, not knowing what to expect. "Athian what is it?" Looking shaken and scared he pointed up to the walls "Demons" "Where Athian, where do you see demons?" "Here in the city, in our supposedly safe haven. They are all over the walls. I saw them moving" There weren't many complete buildings that were still standing but we started to examine those that were. Slowly looking over the buildings we saw nothing but stone walls and statues. Athian again blurted out "There, over there, do you see them? they are moving on the walls." we all looked to where Athian was pointing and that's when we saw the same thing that he did. The statues on the walls were moving, not very much, but the heads of them were slightly moving left to right and up and down "He's right Gideon, I see them also." "The spell worked" said Gideon "They may look like demons but they are not, they are our guardians. The spell has brought life to the statues around us. They are stone guardians, should anything evil or supernatural try to enter past the warding these

Return Of The Bloodstone

will keep them out and the guardians will also stop and fight the hatred of mankind, they will protect us." The city was protected, it had a magical warding and stone guardians to protect us, this was now our safe haven.

Return Of The Bloodstone

Chapter 15

We all now felt more at ease knowing that we had a secure place and stone guardians to help defend us. This didn't however make us feel any more comfortable knowing that we had to leave a safe area and venture back out into danger. "Sloan, you must create a portal to take us to where we need to be." "Gideon, I can't, my portals tend to drop us into random areas." "Nonsense Sloan, if you have seen the area and you have been there then you just think of that area and call forth your portal." Sloan had never tried to summon a portal by thinking of an area before. He thought he would give it a try and while thinking of the settlement and speaking the incantation he called forth a travel portal. Krissy was the first to rush through it and we all then followed her as quickly as we could.

Sloan was the last one to appear on the other-side and once the portal closed he had a look around. "It actually worked, we are here." We found ourselves not far from the settlement and made our way towards it. When we got there we saw what appeared to be the perimeter defences all destroyed and burning or smashed into pieces. The settlement was full of smoke, everything was burning and the skies above us were black, even though the sun was up this area was in darkness. "Why is it so dark" asked Athian. Sloan looked up to the sky before then looking down to the ground. "Darkness has fallen here, the sun will not light these lands and the soil beneath our feet is filled with hatred." We walked slowly though the settlement and noticed that all the buildings had been set alight, we then noticed that all the plant life had wilted away. "We are too late." "What do you mean Athian." "Look" Athian pointed to where the centre of the settlement was and they all saw the bodies of common folk scattered throughout the settlement.

Sloan approached one of the bodies and knelt down to examine it. "They are all drained, all their blood has been drained from their bodies." Sloan then looked at Gideon and asked his master what it meant. "The world is changing, it is changing naturally. We must leave this area." "We need to search the mines" We all agreed with Krissy and made our way up towards the mine entrance. We even saw bodies scattered here as well. All the buildings had been destroyed and everything of use seemed to be taken. They all assumed that the book of magic had been burnt, it was the one thing that Sloan was hoping to find.

We all got to the mine entrance and slowly started to make our way in. "Stop, we cannot enter these mines" "Why not Gideon?" "All the people that were here are dead, Sloan is there anywhere else you can portal us to? Is there anywhere else that you have seen with people that we can save?" Athian decided to speak out before Sloan even had a chance to reply "The village on the east side Sloan, the one where the hunters and fighters were."

Return Of The Bloodstone

We all knew exactly which village Athian was speaking about.

We left the mine entrance and started to make our way to the front of the settlement, Sloan again used the same technique as before, thinking of where he had been and then called forth his portal. We all entered as quickly as we could and we soon found ourselves stood in a village. The village was empty, the people had appeared to of left their homes and had taken what they could with them. "We need to find where they have gone to." "We will Mickel, we will." Whilst walking through the village they soon came across several bodies. "It's too late, they've been here already." After seeing the bodies of common folk Mickel and Athian were both thinking of their home village and hoping the people there were safe.

They assumed that the bodies in front of them were all dead and walked past them as quickly as they could, the smell of rotting flesh was making them feel sick. As they were walking by the decaying corpses they heard a voice muttering in pain. "You must help them, you must find them and help them." looking around the bodies they found one that was still alive, but only just. Large chunks of flesh had been tore from his torso and he had lost so much blood the he was barely able to speak.

In a weak and hoarse voice he told us that the village was attacked by warlocks and witches, he said that they had managed to force them away apart from one, the one with deep burning red eyes. He then unleashed beastly demons into the village. Even though the man was in a lot of agony and struggled to speak he managed to tell us all that he could. He told us the most important thing which was that the common folk were all grouping together and that they were heading towards the mountains. We tried to help the man to his feet but it was pointless. As we picked him up we heard and felt his last breath leave his body.

Now knowing where the villagers were heading to they knew that they had to find them before they reached the mountain. Gideon was a wise man with strong magical abilities. "I can try to find them but it won't be easy." Gideon sat on the ground and crossed his legs with his arms out in-front of him. Muttering lightly to himself we then heard a loud screech from a bird. Looking around to see where it had come from we noticed Gideon had a large golden crested eagle stood beside him. "Oh my god, Mickel look at that." "I can see it Athian." Gideon's eyes had turned to a pure white and the eagle's eye colour had changed to what looked like Gideon's. In an instant the eagle launched itself into the air and started to fly westward.

"Sloan, do we stay here or do we keep moving west?" Sloan looked very decisive of what we were going to do "We keep moving." "No," Shouted Krissy "I'm not leaving him here on his own." They needed to keep moving if they were going to find the common folk and prevent from what they were walking into. "You stay here Krissy, we will head west."   Sloan, Mickel and Athian started to leave the village from the west entrance. Knowing that the villagers were carrying their goods and consisted of elderly and children they knew that they could easily catch up with them. They were quickly able to find tracks from people and carts. They decided to follow them and keep moving as quickly as they could.

Return Of The Bloodstone

The Golden Eagle was soaring high in the sky, scouring all the land down below it. It would fly high into the clouds before gliding downwards, giving itself as much sight of the land as possible. It didn't take long before it was able to find the villagers. They had only managed to get a short distance from the village. The eagle flew down low towards them making sure that it was the common folk. It soared at a safe distance above them and then continued to fly westward. It didn't have to fly far before noticing something else. It had caught sight of Davos and Marcus along with the city guards. Gideon in control of the eagle tried to fly closer to them, he wanted a good look to see what it was that was heading towards the villagers. The eagle was gliding above the evil legion when suddenly a force pulled it fast and hard to ground.

The eagle was unable to fly, the fall to the ground was so hard that it had broken one of its wings. Although it was wounded it managed to get to it's feet and was staggering around the ground, then it felt a sharp pain as an arrow pierced straight through its feathery chest. Back at the village Gideon's eyes suddenly turned back to their natural colour. He rose to his feet sharply before speaking "We need to hurry, quickly Krissy we must go warn the others." "What is it master? what did you see." "I saw what lays ahead of them." They gathered their items and left the village as quickly as they could. It didn't take them long and they soon found the same trail that the other's had found. A trail this easy to find meant that the villagers weren't hiding their movement, they were going to be easy to spot by the enemy that was heading towards them. "Sloan, I see fires burning ahead in the distance." "That's them Athian, we must approach them cautiously, we don't want to startle them." They made their way towards the distant camp-fires. As they approached the camp they heard a whistling cutting through the air. A volley of burning arrows landed into the ground just before them. "Wait, I am Mickel of the Argian Valley. I travel with my friends to speak with the elders." The arrows that were being fired towards them instantly ceased. A single person walked out from the camp and slowly made his way towards them.

The man walked out of the darkness and stood directly before Sloan "did you recover the Bloodstone?" Sloan looked at the man and realised that it was the elder that had sent them on their quest. "Yes we did, It wasn't easy but we managed to recover it." "what decision was made?" Sloan didn't answer right away, he looked across to the boys before looking back to the elder. "A decision was made, we closed the vortex and cleansed the city of evil." "Then the future of our world has been decided." The elder turned around and made his back towards his camp "Follow me."

They sat in the camp around a fire warming themselves up while eating some game food that was offered to them. "What do you think he meant by saying the future of the world had been decided." "I'm not sure Athian, But Mickel chose the world over his own father, possibly to save us all." An expression of relief could be seen upon Athian's face. "Hurry eat Athian, we must go speak with the elders."

They finished their little rest and sought out the elders as quickly as they could. Sloan was trying to explain to them that they couldn't go towards the mountains. The elders were reluctant to listen to him, they had encountered the evil that was now bestowed upon this world and knew that the mountains would offer a natural defence. "You have to listen to me, they have killed all the people at the mountain, the land is dead and dark, all the people there are dead, the same awaits everyone if you go to the mountain." The elders still stood with their decision, "Nowhere is safe, the future of this world has to be decided, and this is our decision.

The elders all gathered together and called forth their people. "We must continue our journey, take all that you can carry and head towards the mountain." No matter how Sloan was pleading to them they weren't listening to him. They all started to leave the camp in groups, each party heading off in the same direction, off towards the mountains that could be seen in the distance. With the elders not listening they tried to warn the people that the mountains were no longer safe, but they had failed in their attempt. The camp was nearly empty and they decided to wait for the arrival of Gideon and Krissy before leaving. They didn't have to wait for long before they soon arrived. "Sloan, where are the elders? where are the people?" "They have gone, they are heading off towards the mountains." "We must stop them" "I've tried master but they aren't listening to me, I've told them that the mountains hold nothing but death." "Death is not at the mountains Sloan, It's just outside of this camp."

As we said this noises in the distance could be heard, sounds of metal striking metal and screams of people in fear and pain. The common folk had walked straight into the path of the city guards. We all quickly ran westwards as fast as we could. We soon caught up to the common folk and could see them in battle against the city guards.

Their arrows were being launched into the advancing lines but they were having little effect, if any at all. They were striking their targets but weren't able to pierce through the now much bloodied armour.

Davos and Marcus could be seen stood at the rear of them all, they were using magic to give the guards extra speed and strength. The sun was was still reaching part of the lands, but not all of it. The city guards had soon reached the mass core of the common folk and one guard stood out amongst them all. He was leading the attack, charging like a wild animal, slicing through the people like they were paper. It was Jax, he showed no fear, no mercy for man, woman or child he didn't care, he was killing them off with ease. His legion of fighters were close behind him and they were trying their best to keep up with him.

"We have to do something" said Krissy "We must help these people and get them out of here." Gideon came up with a plan. "Athian, Mickel, go find the elders, tell them that we have a safe place and they must walk into the light." Krissy asked "What do we do master?" "You two, go stop that giant guard." Mickel and Athian ran through the crowd of retreating people. They found their way to the elders and told them that they have a way to save the people. They didn't want to listen or trust them, but after looking around and seeing what was happening to their people they had to take the risk. Gideon started to create a large travelling portal, he had to stay focussed for as long as he could so they could save as many people as possible.

The portal started to open but no people were going

through it. They saw the effects of magic back in their village and didn't trust it. Mickel and Athian were trying to encourage them, but they still weren't listening. Once the elders started to speak to them and explain that it was safe several of them decided to take the risk. They slowly started to enter and as they disappeared it caused a panic amongst some that were watching. They ran from the portal in fear but what they were running towards was so much worse. It was either through the portal or through the advancing city guards.

Sloan and Krissy were fighting their way through the guards in an attempt to reach and stop Jax from continuing his onslaught. The ground was now covered with the bodies of both common folk and city guards. Luckily for us all the sun was still in the sky and there were no demons in this battle. They could however be seen in the distance with Davos and Marcus just roaming in the shadows. There were no other warlocks or witches with them, it was just Davos and Marcus leading the legion and supporting them with their magical abilities.

Sloan and Krissy had made their way through the city guards and found themselves stood face to face with the legions general, Jax. He towered above them with his blood soaked sword in hand. He quickly swung his sword at Krissy but she managed to evade it, she didn't however evade the backwards elbow that followed it. She was hit hard and fell to the ground. Sloan tried to rush him and tackle him to the ground but he soon also found his laying on the ground in pain as Jax easy knocked him over with his shield. Sloan at this point knew that they weren't going to beat this man by physical force. Jax saw Krissy trying to get to her feet, with his attention now focussed on her he put one foot on her chest pinning her to ground. With his sword in hand and the tip pointing downwards he aimed it right towards her neck. He raised his sword high and just as he was about to thrust it downwards he found himself being pushed backwards through the air. Sloan had managed to save her from what would have been a lethal blow.

"Krissy, quickly get up, I don't know how long I can hold him for." As Krissy was gaining back her senses and was trying to stand to her feet, she noticed a weak point in Jax's armour. "Sloan, hold him back for as long as you can and when I say release him, stop the spell. "Don't do anything stupid." "I know what I'm doing." Krissy positioned herself low to the ground and was inching herself closer towards Jax. "Now Sloan, stop the spell now." Sloan stopped the magical incantation and as he did this Jax found himself rushing forwards at an uncontrollable pace. He was moving too quickly to have full control and as such he lost his footing, he fell forwards to the ground and as he was falling Krissy launched herself upwards from her low stance and with a dagger in her hand she sunk it deep into the underarm of Jax's armour. She managed to thrust her dagger into the weak spot on her first attempt. Jax dropped to the ground rolling in pain and agony. The dagger was so deep in him that he was struggling to remove it. Krissy was shocked to see that it didn't kill him, the dagger sunk so deep that it would of killed most men instantly. They weren't sure what they should do now. Should they leave through the portal with the other's? or should they stay and fight?

The sun was now high in the sky. The ground all

around them could be seen changing, turning from a light brown to a dark black, the corpses that lay upon it could be seen to shrivel, they were being drained, as with the other areas of the world the ground here was also absorbing blood. "We need to go help the others." "No Sloan, let's finish him while we can." A loud noise could then be heard, it was getting louder and louder as they got closer to them. Jax's men were now rushing to his aid. Sloan and Krissy moved themselves away as quickly as they could, there were too many guards coming towards them, they would have had no chance if they decided to fight them off.

Mickel and Athian were getting as many people through the portal as they possibly could. The elders were encouraging all of their people to go through. Gideon was using all his might to keep the portal open for as long as he could. The enemy was encroaching on them very fast. Apart from the elders all the common people were now either dead or had made their way through the portal. Gideon shouted, "quickly, everyone through now." The city guards were now in full control of the battle ground, mankind had lost this battle but managed to escape and survive.

Those remaining turned and were willing to fight against any guards that got too close to them. They could clearly see Jax standing amongst the guards. He had removed his helmet in anger and had showed us his face, guards were not permitted to remove their helmets, by him doing this we all knew that he was infuriated. With Jax revealing his face we all saw that Krissy's facial expression had changed, for the first time we all saw true fear in her eyes. She started to scream and then started to cry.

Gideon shouted out to us "quickly get her through the portal." I knew at this point that they knew this giant guard, I wasn't sure how, but they knew him from somewhere.

All the common folk had now made it through the portal and along with several of the elders. Some of the elders stayed with us in an attempt to fight off the guards. I was struggling to hold Krissy back, she was trying her hardest to go towards the guards that were now rushing towards us. Then the strangest thing happened, we noticed that the daylight was fading. The land had started to get darker, the plants turned brown and were wilting away to dead weeds. the day light was fading. Davos and Marcus were no longer watching on from a distance, they were coming towards us and they were bringing demons with them.

We couldn't understand why the light was fading as we still had several hours of daylight remaining. We looked up to the skies expecting to see the shroud of dark clouds above us once again but there were no clouds to be seen. What we saw was worse, much worse "Sloan, what's happening to the sun." "Everyone through the portal now." They had all quickly made their way through the portal and just as the demons had ran past the guards the portal closed.

We all found ourselves back in the city. We looked around and we saw hundreds of common folk gathered together, all of them were still looking scared. Gideon could be seen speaking to them "You will be safe here, this area is protected from the evil in the world." Many of them that had once escaped the city, now found themselves back within it.

Even though they were now safely stood in the city they still didn't feel secure. They could all see what was in the skies above them. What should be a shining blue sky was now a mixture of black and red. Looking more like an image from hell rather than a normal world. The sun was no longer shining brightly and it's centre was a solid black. Only light coming from the perimeter could be seen. Blaine had succeeded, he had managed to understand the night stone and forced the blackening of the skies by blocking out the sun. We didn't know where Blaine was, or what he was doing, but the world was now in darkness, his darkness. One of the elders walked forth and spoke to us all "So a decision was made, the decision was the wrong one."

Return Of The Bloodstone

Return Of The Bloodstone

Times goes by either in light, darkness or both. What develops over time will always seek to improve and evolve. Should such things be left to grow in the darkness it will only seek to destroy all in it's path, to bring destruction, to bring chaos, to bring death. Those that can survive in such darkness are the hope, the future for all those who live amongst such horrors. As with time knowledge is passed down through generations, with teaching, learning and The Ancient Scrolls. If any were to find the ancient scrolls then they have the power they need, the power to shape the future, or the power to destroy it.

Return Of The Bloodstone

Return Of The Bloodstone